THE BREAKING OF BUMBO

ff

ANDREW SINCLAIR

The Breaking of Bumbo

faber and faber

LONDON · BOSTON

First published in 1959
by Faber and Faber Limited
3 Queen Square London WC1N 3AU
First published in this edition in 1985

Printed in Great Britain by
Redwood Burn Limited, Trowbridge, Wiltshire
All rights reserved

© Andrew Sinclair, 1959

British Library Cataloguing in Publication Data

Sinclair, Andrew
The breaking of Bumbo.
I. Title
823'.914[F]   PR6069.I5

ISBN 0–571–13460–2

TO ANNIE
without whom this book
would *never* have been written

CONTENTS

Part One

The Making of Bumbo

Part Two

Bumbo in Season

Part Three

The Breaking of Bumbo

Part Four

Epilogue

PART ONE

The Making of Bumbo

Green as beginning, let the garden diving
Soar with its two bark towers, to that Day
When the worm builds with the gold straws of venom
My nest of mercies in the rude, red tree.

DYLAN THOMAS: *Altarwise by Owl-light*
in the half-way house

I

BEGINNING IN A BOG

And I don't care who your bleeding fathers are, or how much bleeding money they've got, or what bleeding school you went to—as long as you're here, I'm your bleeding father, and your bleeding mother, and your bleeding school, and you get twenty-eight bleeding bob a bleeding week, just like the bleeding rest of the bleeding bleeders. Bleed it. . . .

Drill Sergeant Plumb, in charge of the Brigade Squad, was welcoming them to Caterham. Bumbo looked at his sweating red face, and chubby five-foot body, which grew twenty-foot high, when he put his ridiculous, straight-peaked, brass-ringed cap on his head, and bellowed. Round Bumbo, sitting on their bare beds, sat the other twenty-three of the Squad, long-haired, public-schooled, frightened, and not showing it.

. . . You're going to hate me like I was the Devil himself, and then, by the time I'm through with you, you're going to love me. Eight weeks, and you'll be loving me. It's happened before, it'll happen again. Now, outside, you bleeding lot, as you are, and the last bleeder out gets the back-end of my pay-stick, up his bleeding backside. . . .

They formed up in threes in the September sun outside, and the drill sergeant began to shout a monologue. Bumbo could not imagine that a man could shout so fast.

. . . Left turn, quick march, left, right, left, right, left, right, faster, faster, you dozy lot, left, right, about turn, about turn, about turn, get a move on you or you'll be in the report, what's your name, tell me after, left, right, left, right, left, right, left turn, left turn, left turn, left turn, right turn, about turn, HALTTTTT. . . . Well, look at you bleeding lot of wasters, form up, bleed you, form up . . . tired eh? . . . out of breath? . . . well, well, you've only just started, stand up, or I'll chase you, till you melt into your boots, you dozy, idle, scruffy lot, I've never seen such a bunch of bleeding wasters in my life . . . stand up, left turn, about turn, left, right, left, right, keep the bleeding step, will you, bleed it. . . .

Etcetera, etcetera, etcetera. Bumbo sweating into his suit, kicking his shoes to pieces on the tar of the paths round the hut, cursing, biting his lip, scared, wondering why the hell he was obeying the moustached pork-butcher, and obeying. Bumbo straining to get breath, straining to stand straight, straining to strain more. Bumbo unthinking, Bumbo one of twenty-four, Bumbo squadded.

They cut off Bumbo's hair, by running a razor up his spinal column, until by the force of its own momentum it ran off the top of Bumbo's skull. *They* crowned Bumbo with a khaki, cardboard dunce's cap, that came off every time he turned round, so that, at the command, he had to run to pick it up, while the others stood at ease. *They* clothed him in uniform that had to be pressed, webbing that had to be cleaned, brasses that had to be rubbed, boots that he had the pleasure of spitting on and polishing afterwards. With an academic flair for mathematical ingenuity, *They* made him fold his bed into a twenty-two inch square each morning, and iron his gym-shorts into a twelve-inch square each evening. *They* made him get up at six in the morning; at eleven at night, he was still sitting in the lavatory, talking with Billy the Kidder, beating the wrinkles out of his best boots with a toothbrush handle. It was only in this sleep-stolen time that Bumbo could remember who he was, or who he had once been.

For *They*, in the seventeen hours daily that *They* had him, Sampson Bumbo, eyeless in Gaza, at the mill with slaves, *They* had cropped his hair, and broken his pride, until it only was in the glitter of his boots. Quarter of an hour for breakfast, half an hour for lunch, half an hour for supper in the evening; drill, rifle drill, field training; the only break in the monotony for five weeks was one game of Rugby, when the Ruddy Reds went down before the Bloody Bogmen; and Bumbo collected such a swollen ankle that he hopped for a week on the Parade Ground on one leg, like a stork on a frozen pond.

His contemporaries seemed to take better to the discipline than Bumbo. Among them, the only crime was to tread on a neighbour's boot, and gossip was a sufficient relaxation. They laughed easily; for anything was funny in their breaking-down. There was loving and laughing Gus, blown backwards, when his tin of

15

Bluebell cleaner, which he was pouring on the coals of the boiler, exploded in his hand. Also Fatboy Jones (who lay on his bed for three weeks believing the Medical Board would fail him as overweight, and then was passed), desperately rubbing his greasy boots with a stubby finger, his greasy boots that would never shine—Fatboy Jones in the report every morning, for unpressed trousers, each night pressing his trousers until he scorched them, and each morning putting them on, only to find that his barrels of thighs blew them out tubular again. Egbert, the Bleeding Waster, that the drill sergeant disliked, saying, Of course, I ain't got a bias against the bleeder, I just hate his guts. Maypole Bean, six-foot seven of honest inability. The Fly Crutcher, the wide-boy manqué, the Sergeant's friend. And the Great Commoner, Outram Utterluck, peerless in title, but also in pride and behaviour.

In fact, Bumbo had known most of them slightly at Eton, where both he and Billy had been Tugs or Collegers, scholarship boys whose brain-power and intellectual snobbery made them isolated, respected and despised by the rest of the school, unless successful athleticism provided a common ground between Tug and Oppidan. Bumbo had been a successful athlete, so the other Etonians, finding Bumbo now approachable, talked with him, and said, Funny, how we know each other here, when we didn't know each other there. And Bumbo said, Yes, funny isn't it; and he did not laugh.

There were twenty-four of them in the Reds, trying for only eight commissions; and twenty-two of them got through the War Office Selection Board for

Officer Training. They had all had a preliminary interview with the Regimental Lieutenant-Colonel, sitting
in his office above Birdcage Walk; and they all knew
that there was a dossier on each of them, in which the
various reports on their progress were put. Bumbo had
been interviewed by the Captain in Command of them;
the Fly Crutcher, needless to say, had managed to see
all the "secret" files on these interviews. Bumbo had
talked on art to the Captain, and, as a reward, had the
following statement under his name. . . . I Like This
Man, But I Find Him Somewhat Quaint and
Eccentric. But Bumbo had passed on to the Officer
Training School, and *They* said that what you did there
was really important.

As the sergeant had prophesied, after six weeks
they began to love him. When they drilled badly, he
chased them in double time, wheeling and turning
them in the late sun, hot as scorched ants, until they
could hardly stand; but, when they drilled well, smack-
ing their heels on the ground one, two, three, four, arms
swinging equally, thirty-inch paces, chin level, rifle
firm on their shoulder, even Bumbo could feel himself,
not as Bumbo solo, but as one of the twenty-four that
were one, that were one under the Drill Sergeant, who
was their father and their mother and their school, as
he had said.

For Drill Sergeant Plumb was a true Man-God.
With his cap on, he roared and thundered like Zeus on
Olympus; but afterwards, when he took off his cap in
the hut, he shrank to the size of the ex-Master Cook.
He told them of his family, of how scared he had been
in the war; he produced eggs which he had lifted from

the cookhouse, like a conjuror, out of his pockets. With the look of a mischievous Billy Bunter, he told them how to get by with the minimum of work; but, with his cap on again, pinching his moustache into imp's horns, he swore that they were getting dozy once more, and he knew what he'd do about that. He praised them sparingly, so that one word of approval clinked in their mind like a medal on their chest. He seemed to think Bumbo a little soft, but he was kind to him, taking his name every day for some offence, and rarely handing it in to the Captain, so that Bumbo got punished less than he deserved.

Sometimes Bumbo, looking at the bare tar, and the bare walls, and the huts that stuck up bare and black against the bare October sky, thought prison would be better than this. It was all a game, playing at being a soldier. For he himself refused to kill; he was a convinced, but silent, pacifist. He had joined the Army as the lesser of two evils; it was unlikely that he would have to fight, in the Brigade, in time of peace. And the thought of going through all the trouble and self-drama of being a *conchie*, rows at his jingoistic home, endless explanations, eternal introspection, jail, made him hold his peace. There didn't seem to be any point in provoking an issue that might never have to be faced. It was, after all, no fault of Bumbo that he was born in a society that accepted conscription gladly, and equated pacificism with treachery. And, at least, to himself, Bumbo was perfectly honest. When the time came, Bumbo would do his duty, and put his conscience before all, even the Brigade. Traitor Bumbo, *They* would say, Turncoat Bumbo. But it was *They* that had put

18

the false colours on Bumbo's back. All men had to cut their coat to fit their cloth, especially to fit khaki or British warm. As long as they knew the truth about themselves, they were all right, Jack.

For what were externals to a Bumbo? He could still go anywhere, do anything, see anyone, like the advertisements in *The Times* of any under-employed modern Proteus. Therefore, temporarily in the wilderness with the wild beasts, Bumbo was a beast too. The forgetfulness of routine shortened every day; the smallness of small talk in his small hut increasingly brought an answer and an interest out of him. Perhaps he would not have *chosen* these people as his friends, but he had to exist with them. If they couldn't talk as he would wish them to talk, he must talk like them. There was something, perhaps, to be learned even among the stupid. Bumbo lived in the day.

It is the midnight before the Passing Out Parade. One high electric-bulb shines as wanly as a cold nose, dripping light from the murk above the lavatories on Bumbo and Billy the Kidder, who are squatting in adjacent bogs talking to each other. Both spit and rub monotonously on the glass and the gloss of the uppers of their boots.

Bumbo says,

Talk of the Slough of lousy Despond. Pilgrims on parade will swab out all bogs, before any Progress is permitted.

Billy says,

Hi, hi, old arty literati you, with Bunyan at

your fingertips, when I've just got my boots. God, I'm tired.

Bumbo says, without listening,

Do you remember that last night before we passed out of Eton, standing in that crummy graveyard outside Chapel, both of us in bloody excelsis ego, so sure we were the tops that we might have been cream on a milk-bottle. Both of us bunged up to the gills with ὓβρις. And look at us now, spitting on a bit of leather in a bog. Talk of the mighty fallen. I bet they didn't get half so low.

Billy says,

I remember. April Fool's day, and all those jokey people put those stag's heads on the Burning Bush, and you got out of the graveyard to have a look-see.

Bumbo says,

That's the night, Kidder. Thinking back on it, it was sort of funny-appropriate. Have you ever thought why they call that old lamp-stand the Burning Bush?

Billy says,

Well, maybe all that scrap-iron round the lamp looks like a privet on fire. Or maybe the designer had a fixation about Moses.

Bumbo says,

Freud. Sexual. The Burning Bush, and there it was, all covered with lovely stag's heads with glass-eyes and succinct epitaphs on their necks like DRUMMANDRACHIT 1909. And *horns*. Masses of horns. Can't you see? Dead significant. The Burning Bush and horns, cuckolds and adultery, holding other men's brats quite sure they're your own. Billy says,

Use it in a script, boy. Very meaningful. But you're going to do a Huxley, not to say an Orwell, aren't you, Bumbolad, before you die?

Billy begins to sing in the semi-dark, improvising,

Dust to dust, and ashes to ashes,
Into the tome the great Bumbo dashes. . . .

Billy laughs at himself, Bumbo says sadly,

I used to think so. I used to *know* so. But I don't know nothing here, except we've got this goddam parade tomorrow.

Billy says,

You'll work out, Bumbo. Take a little of my sincere admiration, for you are the greatest without question writer who never put pen to paper. In fact, zoonds and sdeath, any room for a Boswell, Johnson?

Bumbo laughs. He usually laughs at jokes about himself which he wants to half-believe, in order to disguise that half-belief.

He says,

O.K., Billyboy, confidence restored. The prodigal super-ego has returned home to the id. The fatted boot is roasting on the spit. All's well. But, you know it was funny. I suddenly felt like I was twelve again, all sort of only-child and introspective and isolated-feeling.

Billy declaims,

My heart leaps up when I behold
A Bumbo in the sky.

So was it when my life began;
The child is father to the man,
And Bumbo specially. . . .

Bumbo laughs shortly, and carries on his own monologue,

You know, I even ran away once for a couple of days. But back they took me to The Laurels, Penge. No escape. All that bloody suburbia still makes me sweat, vile villa by viler villa all the way to the Southern Electric station.

Billy says,

Me, I liked trains when I was a kid. Oh, I wanted to be an engine-driver.

Billy sings again,

Daddy wouldn't buy me a choo-choo, choo-choo,
Daddy wouldn't buy one at all. . . .

Bumbo interrupts this song of self-pity for his own pet subject. He says, being tone-deaf and unable to sing,

I reacted against everything. Half-an-hour's religious training a day, and bang, I'm agnostic. Overloaded with mother-love, and now I couldn't care less if I never saw that possessive harpy again. I'm pure rebel through and through. I even changed my name to Bumbo. One might as well get a cheap laugh out of one's own name.

Billy says, mock-serious,

I think Bumbo is the most godawful, clownish, moronic, crummy handle ever fixed to any guy, even to a subhuman like you.

Bumbo says,

That's it. Bumbo the bum. That's me now. Sans hair, sans teeth, sans pride, sans everything. With my beret on, I look like a laid-off lorry-driver. I tell you, Kidder, we're Admass now. We are the Common Man.

Billy says,

Eheu fugaces and all that. Bed, Bumbo, bed. I need sleep ten times as much as you, being nearly normal.

Bumbo says,

Off you go, then. I'll stay and squat me in the shit-house the livelong night, and meditate my toe-caps.

Billy says,

Flush yourself down the plug-hole while you're about it. Night-night.

Bumbo says,

Night.

He hears Billy going, softly, in sneakers, away. He closes his eyes to let the memories of glorious eighteen flap against his eyeballs as nagging and ironic as a blind on a pane in the draught, as hopelessly suggestive as 3-D art studies flicking over in a slot-machine on the pier.

Slide by slide, the pictures with the speaking words tickle and flicker behind his closed lids. Friend Bumbo, walking with Billy round Luxmore's Garden, lost in the utter delight of conscious mutual admiration, striking poses for the benefit of the herd passing by, who envy him in his seeming neglect. Pop Bumbo in sponge-bag trousers, his waistcoat purple with silver buttons, white-tied and lounging, holes in his shoes, while Billy the Beautiful, eighteenth-century flowered brocade between the edgings of his morning-coat, listens to his master. Bumbo, the Experienced One, talks of Life, and, as he talks, he lies.

But Poet Bumbo with Marianne, who is the dream made flesh; eyes, big as brown grapes, lying on the rise of her cheek-bones—fine bones, white bones, that stretch the skin, that push up the swept-back hair a thumb's-length from the eyebrows, that make the nose small as a clenched knuckle, while the bottom lip droops as if a finger had pushed down the hollow of her chin. Dreamer Bumbo, not daring to touch, finding in the precious, true gold. Irrationalist Bumbo, displaying his sensibilities to his love every third day throughout the summer in crested envelopes marked ETON SOCIETY.

> *There is no reason, I tell you, Marianne,*
> > *For death or love:*
> > *Neither can prove*
> *They come for good or bad, as angels can*
> *In allegories. That they come*
> > *Is all their sense,*
> > *Or rather nonsense.*
> *So shall I, must I make my home*
> *Where the sad longings bait the rainy season,*
> > *Light lunatic,*
> > *Gay fantastic,*
> *Beyond the moon. Marianne, there is no reason.*

Then Scholar Bumbo, witty, erudite, effortlessly successful; Scholar of Westminster, Scholar of Eton, Rosebery Scholar, Scholar of Trinity, Cambridge.

Athlete Bumbo, strong, scornful, Grand Old Man; Keeper of the Wall, Golf and Strawberry Mess. Editor Bumbo, Declaimer Bumbo, Actor Bumbo, there was no end to Bumbo's full-face in his past imaginings. For a moment, his capacities seemed again infinite, his possibilities limitless, as in that last term at Eton, when, supertaxed with talents, he bestrode his narrow world like an Onassis. Easy success at school had made him believe that success came easily everywhere; life was an oyster, he the pearl inside it; even while lost in the bog of Caterham, prophet without honour in Army-country, Bumbo was Man and God, for ever and ever Bumbo, Bumbo without end, amen.

Bumbo laughed wryly at his own conceit, and heard himself laughing. He opened his eyes from grandeur to the sad drip of the light. His legs had gone to sleep. He rose, but muzzy pains made his legs feel featherdown so that he had to put one hand on the lavatory-wall to stand upright at all. He swore, but it didn't help the pins and needles in his legs.

Next morning, eight weeks squadded, the twenty-four stood stiffly at attention in the middle of the vast tarmac of the parade ground. A wasp settled on Bumbo's face. Bumbo twitched his nose violently, wriggled his cheek. But the wasp crawled skittishly from his eyebrow down the bridge of his nose to the line that ran from his nostril to the edge of his mouth, giving him the chap-hung look of a melancholy bloodhound.

Drill Sergeant Plumb, dressed in all his glory,

stood in front of the fidgety Bumbo. He snarled,

What's wrong with you, lad? Stop twitching away like a Girl Guide on heat, can't you?

Bumbo twitched still more desperately, as the wasp tickled its path half-way down the huge length of his chin. He spoke out of the corner of his mouth, fearful of disturbing the insect.

There's a wasp on my face, Sarnt Plumb.

Well, lad, did you have your breakfast this morning?

Yes, Sarnt Plumb.

Then don't you be selfish, and let the wasp have his.

A muffled giggle ran along the ranks of threes, and the Drill Sergeant looked pleased. But, taking pity, he stretched out a stubby finger, and flicked the wasp off Bumbo's face. The wasp, however, *en passant*, decided on action, and drove its sting into Bumbo's chin. Bumbo yelled, dropped his rifle, and clapped his hands to his jaw. The rifle, falling, caught the Drill Sergeant in the crutch. A tear ran out of Bumbo's eye, and trickled down Bumbo's cheek.

Well, Drill Sergeant, said the voice of the Inspecting officer.

The Drill Sergeant leapt to the salute, biting on the verbal bullets in the magazine of his mouth. Bumbo, blind with pain, groped for his fallen rifle, and somehow came to attention. The squad stood rigid, waiting for the Judgement Day.

Brigade Squad, all present and ready for your inspection, Sir, shouted the Drill Sergeant.

The Inspecting Officer walked slowly along the

ranks, looking each up and down, and down and up, holding back his comments, like a dog, with the choice of twenty-four lamp-posts to relieve himself on, and undecided which one to try. He stopped in front of Bumbo, who, tear-stained, with eyes tight shut, tried to keep himself still, as ten thousand thorns ran from the agony of his chin.

Ah, said the Inspecting Officer, the acrobat himself. Open your eyes, man.

The officer says, open your eyes, Drill Sergeant Plumb yelled.

Bumbo tried hard to lift up his lids, but they were too tight-shut for his will, and remained closed. He did manage to blink quickly, but he could only see a faint blur, which was the *Deus*-ex-Officers'-Mess of Caterham, before the salt of his tears reduced him to blindness again.

I said, open your eyes, said the Inspecting Officer. Or perhaps, you would like to borrow my handkerchief?

Yes, sir, please, sir, said Bumbo.

Who do you think you're talking to?, shouted the Sergeant. That was a joke, you dozy, idle good-for-nothing you.

Words failed the Sergeant at this point. He took the rifle out of Bumbo's hand, and gave it to the Fly Crutcher. He hissed in Bumbo's ear.

Stand at ease. Stand easy. Pull yourself together. Crying like a babe-in-arms in front of the Commanding Officer. He'll be all right, sir. Carry on, sir, please.

While the two gods moved on, Bumbo wiped his streaming eyes, took back his rifle, and stood to attention once more. But during the drilling that followed, Bumbo lost step, halted late, and tried to salute with his left hand. He preferred to forget the scene that took place that afternoon with the Drill Sergeant, but sometimes, in his nightmares, it used to recur to him, and wake him up, sweating, sitting bolt upright in his bed. He did not know that "Bumbo and the Wasp" was the Inspecting Officer's funny story for a month and a half afterwards, until the ice on the parade ground brought down half the recruits on a particularly sharp right turn in December. In fact, Bumbo left the barracks in misery, and in sadness, only sure that still, in himself, he was unchanged. But, afterwards, looking back at his breaking, he knew that the crust from outside had begun to harden into his skin at the Depot. Bumbo was no longer what he *knew* he was. O Bumbo that was God, O Caterham.

2

SET FOR A SEDUCER

Bumbo took Marianne to *Porgy and Bess* during the week's leave he had between Caterham and Eaton Hall, the Officer's Training School. The spell was still there, the love, the dream, garden and maiden, but Bumbo of the Brigade had learned more, heard more, thought he needed more. Marianne kissed his cheek at the end of the evening, and said,

You haven't changed at all, Bumbo. Don't please.

Bumbo boasted,

I'll change the Brigade.

But he had to learn. A whore would have been the best; but then there was the disease. So it had to be a fool, then. A débutante would be most convenient. For luckily he had been asked to an out-of-Season dance, given for the sister of one of his Brigade acquaintances, the night before he left for the North.

The dinner-party gives Bumbo what he wants. Her name is Sheila—shop girl's name. She is small, dark-haired, naïve to the point of pity. Yes, she is coming out next Season.

Bumbo gives her no chance to escape at the dance. For two hours, he guards her, making her drink too much with him. She is flattered by her first conquest. A flush makes her face red. She talks faster.

Bumbo Seducer looks at her, smiling. It is one o'clock. They are dancing a waltz.

Bumbo says,

There are too many people here, Sheila. Let's go.

Where?

Bumbo sees Sheila blushing at the innocence of her remark.

Carnival suit you?

Yes.

In the taxi, Bumbo takes Sheila's hand in his. For a little while, he does not squeeze, and, after the first limp pull away from him, she leaves her hand in his. Bumbo tries desperately to be amusing, but her laughter is only dutiful, nervous. Luckily, it is not far to Piccadilly.

In the Carnival, Bumbo plays it along the line. They are shown to a table against the wall below a vague light shining through a vase. Five couples are dancing cheek-to-cheek, five sit at the close-set tables. Harry is singing suggestive songs at the piano. The couple next to them are kissing each other. A waiter comes near.

Bumbo says,

What will you have? Shampoo or gin?

Shampoo, if. . . .

Oh, yes. So glad we've missed the cabaret. It's usually pretty poor here.

Bumbo had only been to the Carnival once before, when he had enjoyed the Greek, French and English songs of a bearded sailor.

Bumbo says,

Shall we dance?

Yes, please.

Sheila edges to the floor, and waits for Bumbo. He sees her indecision, and holds her hard against him. For a minute he dances with her, talking. Then, naturally, slowly, he puts his cheek against hers. They shuffle hip to hip, leg between leg, for ten minutes round the full eight-yard square of the dance-floor.

Bumbo says,

Shall we sit?

Sheila nods.

They sit, and the waiter brings a bottle of champagne over to their table. At the pop of the cork, Bumbo thinks of his cheque-book, makes a wry smile.

Shampoo, Sheila dear?

Thank you.

Bumbo edges closer to her on the narrow plush of the seat.

Tell me, what do you think of your first night-club?

How do you know it's my first?

I shouldn't have brought you, if I hadn't known. After all, night-clubs are only enjoyable for the first time. Our boredom is their *raison d'être*, and yet they only increase it.

Sheila laughs dutifully, as though she understood.

Bumbo says,

Let's dance again.

The atmosphere of the Carnival is hot. Bumbo and Sheila get up, shuffle, squeeze, hug, sweat a little, sit down. Sheila is drinking more of the champagne than Bumbo. She smiles at him. He turns his face downwards, and kisses her on the shoulder.

Sheila says,

Not now. Later.

It is half-past three, and they have finished their bottle of champagne. There is only one other couple left in the Carnival. Harry has sung his final song, but he still plays, hoping that they will go. Bumbo nods towards the floor.

Last time?

Yes.

Sheila sways slightly, as she stands up. She puts her arms round Bumbo's neck. He locks his hands round her waist.

Bumbo says,

Do you love me?

Sheila says,

Yes.

Bumbo kisses her on the lips; they are soft and slack, so that he finds that he is rubbing his mouth on her teeth.

Bumbo says,

Let's go now. Where are you staying in London?

Sheila says,

Sloane Square. At a friend's flat. But she's away in the country. I didn't tell mamma that, or she wouldn't have let me come to the dance.

Bumbo says,

She's a useful friend. Come, I'll see you home.

In the taxi, Sheila sprawls uncomfortably across Bumbo. At intervals, between the traffic-lights, they continue to rub mouths. Bumbo carefully murmurs broken words of endearment, trying to remember what *They* say in women's magazines. A cold happiness fills his mind, a logical joy, as if he were solving a crossword-puzzle.

He gets out of the taxi with Sheila, pays the driver, and says,

Let's have one final drink, and make plans.

Sheila says,

Yes, Bumbo darling.

Bumbo has almost to carry her up the stairs. The living room of the flat is large, the sofa as big as a bed. Sheila lies on the sofa.

Bumbo says,

Where are the drinks?

Over there, on the shelf.

Bumbo pours out a large gin for Sheila, and a small one for himself. He brings back the drinks, slopping them on the carpet, although his hands are steady.

Bumbo says,

Darling, knock this back in one, and I'll kiss you.

Sheila giggles,

What are you doing? Do you want to make me drunk?

Bumbo says,

You've got much too hard a head for that.

Sheila swallows the drink in a gulp, and says,
Darling, kiss me.
Bumbo puts an arm round her, places his mouth on hers, tastes the ginny smell of her breath. Sheila now opens her teeth, and Bumbo runs the tips of his lips along their edge. His hands press into her bare shoulders. Inside himself, he feels nothing, nothing at all.
Darling, Sheila says.
They lie side by side on the sofa. Bumbo is looking for progress. His hands fumble uselessly, pretending that they are caressing. He wants to undress her, but he doesn't know how. Which hooks what? What zips where? Where pins which? The whole thing is bloody ridiculous.
Bumbo says,
Darling heart, I should go.
Sheila hugs him tightly, then relaxes tiredly,
Not yet, sweetie.
They lie for another quarter of an uncomfortable hour. Then Bumbo rolls over on to his side to look at the clock on the table.
Sweet, it's nearly five. I really must go.
Sheila looks up at him. Her face is red and blotched.
You're not catching a train till half-past six. You can stay here till then, if you want to.
Bumbo calculates, and says,
But you're getting up early too. You need some sleep.
Sheila yawns,
You come and tuck me up. My God, I feel tired.

Bumbo picks her up in his arms, carries her into the bedroom, staggering, and puts her on the bed. He goes back to the door to switch on the light. Sheila rolls onto her stomach, and tries to unhook the back of her dress.

Bumbo says,

I'll help you.

He begins slowly unfastening the bent wires. There is a red line indented on her body, where the top of the dress has been, then puckered skin, then a white strap, then more skin. Sheila is breathing heavily, and Bumbo can smell the gin. His stomach tenses. He looks at the white ceiling, then at the chintz flowers on the curtains. There is a gilded cupid on the dressing-table by the wall.

Sit up, Bumbo says.

He pulls her upright. Lines are notched by her eyes, her mouth slack as a slipped bow-string. She murmurs,

Want to go to sleep. What's matter? Love you.

Bumbo shakes her backwards and forwards, while the bed-springs creak, filing against the wood, as if the situation had developed normally.

You don't love me, you fool. You don't. You don't.

Bumbo throws her flat, back on the blankets. He sits, looking through the half-open door into the living room. He says,

Splendid, aren't I. Bloody wonderful. Get a sweet fool, fill her with drink, take her to the Carnival, bring her home, and . . . oh god, bloody Bumbo Hero.

Sheila, sagged on the bed, says,

Love you.

Bumbo goes over to the basin, and fills a tooth-glass with water. He stands over the bed, looks at Sheila for a few seconds. She has closed her eyes. He tilts the glass.

Blast you, says Sheila.

She sits up, putting her hand to her head. She begins to cry. The top of her dress falls down. Her underclothes are wet. Bumbo sits down beside her, holds his arm round her, and says,

Don't cry, darling.

Sheila looks up at him, scared, drawn, white.

I'm going to be sick, she says.

Bumbo watches her go to the basin.

Afterwards—conventionally afterwards—Bumbo wraps her in her dressing-gown, and makes her sit on the sofa in the living room. He goes into the kitchen to make some tea. Sheila comes in after him.

Bumbo, I'm so ashamed. What do you think of me?

Nothing. I don't think anything.

They drink the tea from beer-mugs, sitting side by side on the sofa.

Bumbo says,

I feel just as bloody as you. It was all my fault.

There is a silence.

Bumbo says,

I'd better be going.

Sheila says,

Yes.

Bumbo goes.

3

GREEK AGAINST BARBARIANS

Marathon was a rocky hillside, in January, under snow. "D" Company had come out in trucks early that morning to take up positions on the hill for a 48-hour exercise against "C" Company, two miles away, on the hill opposite, across the valley.

Bumbo and Maypole Bean were given a site, where they were meant to dig their trench. They spent all that day digging. They managed to penetrate six inches into the ground, which was solid rock. They dug the trench in the shape of a T, so that, by lying with their legs at a right angle to their trunks, and sleeping, faced outwards, bottom to bottom, they could both squeeze into one half of the T of the trench. That evening the snow melted, and Bumbo's bed became the main drain. He spent the night standing; water had soaked through six of his seven layers of clothing. The rest of the Brigade Squad squatted under their structure of earth and corrugated iron, and drank the rum they had brought with them. The trogs (the other Officer Cadets, exclusive of the Greenjackets), suffered without alcohol.

During the next day, "C" Company staged an

attack, and captured a prisoner. It was necessary for "D" Company to send out a patrol that night to capture a prisoner in return. The Officer-in-Command chose Bumbo to act as Platoon Commander, and to lead the patrol.

Bumbo briefed his patrol. With him were the Fly Crutcher, a Marine Novice Heavyweight Boxing Champion, and six nondescripts. Bumbo's plan was, by any standard, hazy; but he relied on the good visibility to lead him to the enemy position. They were to start at two. At ten, thick fog rolled up from the valley.

The patrol did start at two. The Captain, who was coming with them as an observer, was swearing. Bumbo could see as far as his own elbow, and no farther. He looked hopelessly into his compass, and suddenly remembered that he had forgotten to learn how to read it. He set off into the fog. After five paces, the ground gave way under his feet. Earth fell, tin buckled, and Bumbo found himself sitting on the drunk face of Outram Utterluck, who was slumbering at the bottom of his trench. Bumbo climbed out, and set off again.

One hour later, Bumbo was lost, badly lost. Every ten minutes, the Captain said, Are you sure you know where you are, Bailey?

Yes, said Bumbo stubbornly, and blundered on.

This was the important exercise. From those who distinguished themselves. four Junior Under Officers were chosen to lead the platoons. The Reds would certainly take, among their eight vacancies, any of their candidates who became an Under Officer.

The fog began to lift a little, as a steady rain set in. Bumbo could now see a couple of yards in front of himself. Like indigo spirals in a black marble, lumps of mist hung, isolated, in the thick night. Every thirty yards Bumbo made his patrol halt, and lie down, legs touching, on the morass below them. This was what the textbooks specified, although it was obvious that only mad dogs and soldiers would be out for a stroll in this midnight limbo.

The Captain spoke,

Are you sure you know the way, Bailey?

Quite sure, sir, said Bumbo sincerely.

He squinted for form's sake into his compass again, turned sharply to his right, took sixteen paces, tripped over a wire, and fell flat on his face. He sat up, holding the wire in his hand. It was the enemy's ground telephone line, that ran from the forward position of their scouts to their Company Headquarters.

Eureka, said Bumbo.

He kept his hand on the magic thread of wire, and followed it in through the fog. Theseus Bumbo, *en route* to the Minotaur.

A light was suddenly shining up into the night. They dropped on their bellies. They heard an angry voice talking.

What the hell are you doing with that light in the middle of the night? Put it out, you fool.

The voice of Mad Taffy replied; he was the unlicensed buffoon of "C" Company.

I'm looking for airyplanes, bach.

They lay quiet for five minutes, until there was no noise. They crawled forwards, and came to a hole in

39

the ground. Bumbo sent the Marine and the Fly Crutcher into the hole. He heard a conversation, a dull thud, and a small scream. Behind him, five yards away, someone spoke.

Who's that?

Bumbo turned. The night was clearing now. Through the rain, Bumbo could see Squich, a pathetic figure, whose uncle commanded Billy's regiment, the Scarlets. He had a rifle in his hand, and was obviously playing at sentries.

Bumbo growled,

Bleed off, bleed you.

Squich walked off quickly, scared to hell he had offended his own side. The Marine and the Fly Crutcher reappeared from the trench, meekly followed by the prisoner.

Well done, Bumbo whispered.

Tcha, said the Fly Crutcher. I spoke sweet reason in one ear, and Old Bigfists landed him one on the other. He's as quiet as mamma's little lamb.

The patrol set off for home. The prisoner, once he had lost sight of his own positions, was so scared of being deserted in the middle of the godforsaken, howling, soaked lostness, that, even when they ignored him, he tagged along behind.

A quarter of a mile to the North of "C" Company's trenches was the Scarp, a five-hundred foot sheer drop, down to the valley. Bumbo came to the slope that ran down to the edge of the cliff. He stopped, knowing at last where he was, and unrolled his map, lighting it with his flash-light. The way back seemed simple. Across the top, down the slope, over the valley, up the far hill. Bumbo rolled up the map, switched off the light.

Forward, Bumbo said.

At half-past four, one and a half hours later, Bumbo and the patrol were still at the edge of the Scarp. In fact they had been round in seven complete circles, always coming back to their starting-point. They had stumbled across the tent of the "C" Company officers, cut the guy-ropes, and put thunder-flashes inside. But otherwise unsuccessful, they were so tired and waterlogged from the continual rain that they were complaining audibly. Bumbo had a fit of night-blindness, unable to see at all for long intervals, walking into trees, falling, always walking on, des-perately, suddenly, in a panic. And they were still at the Scarp.

The Captain, who had settled into a sullen silence, now spoke,

Well, Bailey, shall *I* take you home?

No, sir, said Bumbo.

Desperation dulled in his skull.

Shortest way home, Bumbo said. Follow me.

He began to walk down the slope towards the edge of the Scarp. It was only five-hundred foot straight down, and then they were all ruddy well in the lousy valley.

Stop, Bumbo heard the Captain call behind him. For God's sake, stop, Bailey.

Bumbo went on.

Stop, stop, Bailey, stop . . . Bumbo, for God's sake.

Bumbo stopped.

You can't go that way.

Oh, said Bumbo, I suppose I can't.

He couldn't think any more. His clothes were sogged down, like thick, soft callouses on his skin. He couldn't think. He just stood.

I'll take you back, as far as the valley anyway.

Bumbo dragged after the Captain in silence. In ten minutes they had reached the valley.

I can take over from here, Bumbo said.

All right, said the Captain.

Bumbo led the patrol across the valley, and up a slight slope. They came to a strand of wire-netting, with a red triangle hung upon it.

Minefield, said the Captain. You've got to go round.

At lousy five o'clock, said Bumbo inaudibly, in the lousy morning, how come we're still playing lousy games, pretending that there are lousy mines in a lousy field full of lousy cowpats.

Forward, men, he said audibly.

Bumbo followed the outside of the barbed-wire, and found himself again in the valley.

Bumbo wept.

The rain stopped. It began to freeze.

I'll take you back by the road, said the Captain.

At half-past five, Bumbo was standing in the tent that served as Company Headquarters. The Officer Cadet, chosen to play at Company Commander for the duration of the exercise, sat there with his staff. They were interrogating the prisoner, who, bored as hell, told them everything they wanted to know.

Can't we go to sleep now? he said.

No, he couldn't. Bumbo could see the Cadet-playing-Company-Commander wanting so badly to be an Under Officer. It wasn't any good. He didn't make it anyway.

Bumbo sat on the floor, and spent half an hour trying to take off his boots. He took off his socks too, wrung the water out, put them back on, and his boots also. The rest of the patrol went off to find dry clothes, except for one nondescript, who went to sleep in the tent without changing, and woke up frozen, got gangrene in his feet, and had to stay two months in hospital.

Bumbo stood up. The weather was so lousy that the Army had issued duty rum. There was a full bottle on the table. Bumbo took a swig. He felt sodden through to his bones. The rum in his mouth tasted like warm water. Bumbo took another swig, supporting himself with one hand on the table. In ten minutes, Bumbo finished the bottle.

It was six o'clock. Time for Bumbo to call his platoon, to tell them to fill in their trenches, and to report for breakfast at seven, ready to march ten miles back to the Hall at eight. Bumbo turned to go. He fell over. He picked himself up, and took another step. He fell over again.

You all right, Bumbo?

Yup, said Bumbo, and fell out of the tent.

Bumbo's platoon position was a couple of hundred

yards away up a slope. The path there, which had been a stream in the rain, was now a strip of ice, slipping between fences of barbed-wire.

Every two or three steps that Bumbo took, he fell over. He felt no pain, only surprise. Often he fell into the barbed-wire, and rose, listening to the tearing of his uniform and hands with apathy. He must have fallen fifty times going up the hill. Sometimes he crawled, as it was less trouble. He fell for the last time into the forward trench of his platoon.

The white face of Laughing Gus paled the gloom. The smell of stale rum, damp and brandy flapped in Bumbo's nose.

Bumbo heard his tongue moving in his mouth. He was in command of his men, if not of his faculties.

Sorry, Gus, but I'm drunk, tight as a tic, tac, toc . . . you've got to get up now, fill in your trench . . . so sorry I'm so drunk, but you've got to be moving, breakfast at seven, march off at eight . . . and, Gus, I'm very drunk, you see, I didn't mean it. . . . . . . so be an angel, and take me to the next trench . . . can't stand up . . . isn't it funny. . . .

Bumbo slapped his own face, hard.

. . . There . . . behave . . . Gus, be an angel, and give me a hand. . . .

Gus helped him out of the trench, and dropped him into the next one, where he repeated his message, and was taken on, trench by trench, all round the position, treading behind his helpers infinitely carefully, with the tedious caution of the drunk.

At seven o'clock, Bumbo sat under a tree, on the last remaining patch of snow. He stuffed the snow into the hollow of his helmet, and put the pack on his face. He did not look more beautiful.

A kind trog packed up his bedding for him, and took it down to the truck. Bumbo, staggering down the path, a mess-tin in each hand, fell over less often now; but, as he came to the three Captains, who stood side by side, watching the Officer Cadets eat their breakfast, he fell over once more.

Sorry, said Bumbo.

He picked himself up.

A cook took him by the shoulder, sat him by the fire, and put a cigarette in his mouth. Bumbo let it fall onto the ground. The fire melted the ice on the outside of Bumbo's clothes. A puddle formed at his feet. With a fork, Bumbo ate a little of the spaghetti out of his mess-tin. He looked up, to find his Captain standing over him.

Bailey, said the Captain, you're literally blue in the face. You're all in. You'd better take the truck back.

I'm all right, Bumbo said. I'll walk.

The Captain went away. Bumbo sat dull and heavy for a long time. Then he walked to the road, and stood by his platoon, which had formed up without him.

He heard the platoon in front of him begin to march.

Number 16 Platoon, croaked Bumbo. Quick March.

Bumbo marched along the road. Left, right, left, right, left, right. His body was no longer part of him. The toe of one boot followed the heel of the other, and Bumbo watched them move, and could not understand. Muzzily through his mind, recurrent, two sentences beat again and again at the plod of his heels on the ground. Bumbo drunk. Bumbo busted. Bumbo drunk. Bumbo busted. It was like a marching tune. Bumbo drunk. Bumbo busted. No, Bumbo wasn't Bumbo any more. He was just a moving, marching thing that *They* called Bumbo. He had a number, 74038647; sometimes he had a name. But his identity was now a disc on his neck; he could take it out, and look at it, and see only a flat, circular, almost two-dimensional area of plastic, with the superscription,

74038647
BAILEY, B. J.
RED. GDS.

Bumbo looked at his being, strung so conveniently under his sodden clothing on a string round his neck. Then he put his identity away. If that was all Bumbo was, it could stay wet on his chest. Just now he was concerned with left after right, right after left. Bumbo drunk. Bumbo busted. Left after right, right after. . . .

Bailey, get in here with me, said a gin-deep voice.

Bumbo lifted his head, and looked to his left. There, pop-eyeing out of the window of his car, was the round, fat, piggy, bloated, blood-veined face of the Mad Major, who commanded "D" Company. *They* said he had been seconded from Kenya for ill-treating the Kikuyu. That's why, by Christ, as he often said, DOG Company was going to be the best bloody Company in the place. He wanted to get back to Regimental Duties, by distinguishing himself at the Hall. And so he drove them on, helped by his sadist Sergeant-Major, a Scarlet, shell-shocked in the war, so that pain sometimes turned him into a maniac. His second week at the Hall, Bumbo had only averaged two hours sleep a night, and had nearly stuck a bayonet into himself, under the incessant, neurotic shouting of the Scarlet Sergeant.

The Mad Major puffed,

Bailey, you look done in. Get in this car with me, and I'll drive you back.

Bumbo looked at the yellow scum of nicotine that edged the Major's mouth. A scrap of paper had stuck itself to his lip.

Bumbo said,

I'm all right.

The scrap of paper worked itself up and down below the fatuous moustache. The Mad Major spoke again.

I know what's right for you, and what's wrong. Get in, Bailey.

Bumbo stressed his words carefully,

I *said* I was *all right*. I'm *walking*. I *want* to *walk*.

The Mad Major looked redder, if that was possible.

BAILEY, do you HEAR me? GET IN. This is an ORDER. GET IN.

Bumbo said, as quiet as desperation,

Bleed off, will you?

Bumbo walked on. Behind him he heard the Mad Major let in the clutch. The car accelerated past him. His platoon looked at him. He shrugged, and walked

47

on. That had done it. Bumbo drunk. Bumbo disobeying an order. Bumbo telling his Commanding Officer to bleed off. Bumbo busted. Bumbo busted so hard that he spends the rest of his eighteen months peeling potatoes in Aldershot. Bumbo drunk. Bumbo disobedient. Bumbo busted. Bumbo marched, left foot after right, and right foot after left, ten miles to the Hall.

The next morning, the Mad Major held a post mortem on the exercise. Bumbo, waiting for the inevitable, had packed his kit in his kitbag, ready to depart. He sat at the back of the room.

The Mad Major was frothing,

Boys, I'm proud of you. Proud of Dog Company. It's the best bloody Company in the whole bloody Hall. And what makes me especially proud is guts. You've got guts. Nobody has got so much guts as you. It's guts that count, and you've got them. Guts. I won't mention any names, but there's one of you has really got guts. There he was, out on his feet, and I offered him a lift, and he told me, your Commanding Officer, to bleed off. Me, to BLEED OFF. Haw, haw, haw. TO BLEED OFF. Didn't know he knew such a word. Haw, haw, haw. . . .

The audience laughed respectfully. Bumbo laughed respectfully too. It seemed to be the fashion. Then Bumbo realized that the Mad Major was talking about him.

And the Captain followed on behind the Mad Major, and praised Bumbo's finding of the enemy by tripping over the wire as the smartest bit of fieldcraft he had ever seen.

So the farce ended, with Bumbo the Drunk as Bumbo Hero. In the Army's opinion, he was bunged up to the pips with officer-like qualities, and if the Army didn't know what officer-like qualities were, who did? Perhaps being an officer was getting drunk, and still being able to walk. Bumbo staggered out to relieve himself, and considered his reflection for a long time in the mirror over the washbasin. He then rapped his nose in the glass. He saw why they had been taken in.

You're a naughty old man, he said to himself. It's a lovely mug, a Jesus Q Christ mug, looking like it's bearing the sins of several worlds. But they didn't ought to believe it. I don't. Still, roll on. Bleeding roll on.

Bumbo became an Under Officer, and went with his Company for a fortnight's field training down in Devon. Billy was there also. He was not doing well at the Hall, and had never been near being made an Under Officer. The old patron-and-client relationship of Bumbo and Billy, the joking-relationship of the bog, came back in the long evenings, drinking beer and mead in the pubs of Okehampton and Hatherleigh, after the endless slogging over the moors in the day-time. It was in this fortnight, that Bumbo once again found himself one in his body, now grown hard and strong. Again he knew that everything was possible for a Bumbo, even as a soldier. And if the other Etonians now resented his authority over them, he seemed to be liked by the trogs. They often said to him that he was not really one of the Brigade, that he was truly Bumbo Unique, the only one among them that they did not mind as their leader. The Brigade resented his declared preference for the trogs to them, and baulked at his authority; but, when he gave an order, they obeyed him. The image of Bumbo at Eton still lingered in their minds, Bumbo the Great; and if that image had been melted down with them into the mould of sameness at Caterham, yet Phoenix Bumbo had risen again from the ashes, not beyond question now, but still set in authority over them.

Marianne wrote that she was going to be married. Bumbo wrote back, heroic, sacrificial, self-dramatic, and abandoned himself to a mood of gentle melancholy. Time seemed to be waiting for him. The past was irretrievably gone, even although he could recapture faint glimpses of what it had been in soporific, beer-heavy conversations with Billy. His trick of disassociation, when he was sober, seemed to make his previous faith in himself naïve; and, although he did not doubt his success to come, he saw that glory would now be a matter of waiting. The Brigade around him all seemed so secure in their stupidity. They knew that they had houses, money, power, the black-and-blue tie; that they were the salt of the earth, this was never a matter of doubt to them. They were born great. They did not need, in the Army, the greatness of a Bumbo to be thrust upon them.

Billy left a week earlier than Bumbo for his last fortnight at the Hall. Bumbo spent the remaining week-end in a small pub, on the other side of the moor, alone. His life was such a series of compartments now, all various and unrelated, megalomania at Eton, humiliation at Caterham, London for laughs and Eaton Hall for stupidity, that Bumbo felt badly the loss of one of his two binding-threads, Billy and Marianne. Moreover, he thought the occasion demanded a last poetical expression. But now the writing of poetry came hard, and, when it did come, it had the air of such contrivance that Bumbo sent his signing-off note more as a duty to Marianne, who expected it, than in the belief that it was Forlorn Lover Bumbo really signifying the true nobility of his emotions.

> *I ask for mead at a Dartmoor Inn*
>   *That I chance to pass*
> *They call the drink Sack Methaglin,*
>   *Or Hippocras,*
> *Or Melomel or Bochet. And I find*
>   *That I remember*
> *A girl, whose heart is the grey wind*
>   *Of December,*
> *Whose voice is heather-honey, and whose eyes*
>   *Are honey-brown.*
> *And I go coldly to the low skies*
>   *Beyond Blackdown.*

In fact, Bumbo had never been near Blackdown. It was the low o-sound in the name, with its double staccato thump that had made his inspired sensitivity remember the word. He rather thought that Blackdown was, actually, a prison, or a camp for Sappers.

Bumbo arrived back at Eaton Hall on the night of the dance, that took place three times a year. A band had been bribed to sit in the appalling draughts of the Hall, that vast mock-Gothic railway station *manqué*, which stuck out signal-arms of pinnacles to control the nissen huts, clustering like locomotives between its gold-yellow sides and the fantastic imitation of Cleopatra's Needle, that some lunatic aristocrat had erected half-way down a tarred avenue.

Apparently, the Scarlet Sergeant had been around at tea-time to announce those who had been accepted into the Brigade, and those who had failed. Bumbo was in; he was stationed in London to perform Public Duties; but Billy had been turned down. He now sat on his bed in the Chinese Suite, backed by a bright frieze of humming-birds and verdigris-green. He did not speak. Bumbo knew that Billy's father had been killed in the Regiment in the war. He knew that Billy's mother had set her heart on his joining. He did not know what to say. It seemed so stupid that he, who did not care, should get into the Reds with such ease, and that Billy should fail.

Bumbo speaks,

Let's go and get a drink, Billy. You know, you're lucky really. I should think a County Regiment's a hell of a relief. Anything to get away from the all-Etonians-together atmosphere.

Billy the Kidder smiles, and says,

It was all for a Redcoat, mother,
That I laid me down to die.

Bumbo says,

It doesn't matter, Billyboy. It's probably a blessing in khaki. Much more fun.

Billy says,

Sure, sure. Me, I'm an optimist.

Bumbo says,

Come on, Kidder. Let's go and have a brown in the NAAFI.

Billy came with him to drink in the NAAFI. They talked, as they had always talked before, of Bumbo, and of Billy and Bumbo. Then they went back to the Hall, and sat in chairs outside the dance.

Girls passed, girls that were shivering, their wraps round their shoulders, pretending that it was all so gay, such fun, quite, quite heaven. Only fools would have been taken in by their pretence, but fools were with them, and laughed, and shouted to each other,

. . . God, you're stinking!

Don't you think she's a hell of a fruit?

Genial totties, eh?

Are you sure you won't have another drink? Just a teeny-wee one. . . .

Gosh, what a LOVELY place, it looks so OLD. . . .

Yes, that *was* my foot, actually. . . .

Really. . . .

Truly. . . .

Promise me. . . .

Ecstatically. . . .

Angelically. . . .

For ever and ever, my darling. . . .

They move fast, but so heavy, so red. Occasionally one of the men shouts to Bumbo and Billy, or gives them his glass of champagne. But Bumbo and Billy sit inside the bubble of their isolation, together as usual in Bumbo's success, again in the quarantine of their mutual admiration, excluding the abominable healthy. As in the bog, Bumbo talks of himself, sure that Billy understands that his consolation consists in being made to share in Bumbo's triumph.

Bumbo says,

They're all so *fixed*, these gawping, stuffy faces. They're such a Godforsaken lot—if He ever went there in the first place. They're restricted to two expressions for use in company, the Polite Interest, and the God-I'm-Happy. The first, lips closed, left eyebrow slightly raised, hand on hip, gaze intent, and the posture slouched. The second, lips parted to show twenty-four English teeth, both eyebrows burned off by misfires from cigarette-lighters, hands on other people's hips, gaze besotted, and posture still slouched but in motion. Any more for any more?

Billy is strangely silent. He just says, No, I can't think of any.

Bumbo says,

Masks. That's all they wear. No flesh underneath. Funny, when I was a kid. . . .

Bumbo thought he heard Billy groan, but it must have been the sound of a champagne-cork.

. . . I used to make up a world of my own. I'd sit up in the attic, and I'd have five masks I'd bought at the toy-shop, and I'd put them on, and I'd speak to myself with different voices. I remember, I really thought they were proper people. They all had names, characters, the lot. There was the Slick Sheik, sort of slimy like a snail. Then Buffo the Brown Clown, always capering around to the sound of soundless barrel-organs. And the Beater, just the same type as the Mad Major. Then Thistlethought, who was a bit of all that's nasty, intelligence and prickles. And the last was the product of my super-Christian indoctrination courses, Suffering Cerberus, who was green, and always spoke Categorical Imperatives in capitals, rumbling away in a pulpit-bass. But my father burned them all one day, said I was wasting my time. I cried a lot, but I guess I had to make do with my own face after that.

Billy yawns,

Imaginative kid, weren't you. But always *your* imagination. God, I'm tired. I think I'm off to bed. It's been bloody exhausting, up here.

Bumbo says,

I think I'll have just one more drink. You are feeling all right about it all now, aren't you? I mean, you're not going to go off and shoot yourself, or something.

Billy points two fingers wearily at his temple, and says,

Bang, bang. I'm dead. Lie down and count ten, or I won't play with myself any more.

Bumbo laughs,

You're always playing with yourself, you old Kidder.

Billy sings with a twisted mouth,

Bye, bye, black sheep, have you any wool?
Yes, sir, yes, sir, three bags full. . . .

Nighty-night, cheerio, chippy chip, R.I.P. and see you never.

Bumbo says,

Pip, pip, Emma.

Billy goes away, up the stairs. Bumbo wanders into the dance to chatter and drink with the others. He is bored. He decides to go up and see Billy before he gets to bed. He goes up the stairs to the Chinese Suite. The door will not open. Bumbo runs against it, once, twice, three times, pushing back the weight that holds it shut. He squeezes into the room, and goes round the tin locker that has been put against the door. Billy is lying on the bed. A rifle is on the ground by his side.

Bumbo shouts, Help.

Finished? says Billy. He sits up.

For Christ's sake, he says, can't you leave me alone?

Bumbo says,

I thought . . . I thought you had shot yourself.

Billy sneers. It is the first time Bumbo has seen Billy sneer.

Nothing so dramatic. Sorry to disappoint. But it's no thanks to you that I haven't. None at all. Of course, I'm not *sad* or anything, oh no, I'm not miserable, I mean one fails to get into the Scarlets every day of the week. But I might have killed myself out of sheer boredom. I just get so bloody bored listening to you talking about your bloody self. Everything's a personal question. There's nothing else, just you. I might be feeling any bloody way, mad, gay, extrovert, intelligent, but however the conversation begins, it always ends with you. So it always ends with you. And me too.

Bumbo says,

I do understand you're feeling a bit low now. You'll be all right in the morning.

Billy says,

Oh, no. No, no. I've had enough, bloody basta. I'm just going to be me, not who you think I am or who you want me to be. I'm buzzing off in a week to a little, dull, ordinary County Regiment where nobody's going to read me lectures, or tell me sermons, or make me watch them showing themselves off as examples of everything.

Bumbo says,

Hi, Kidder. What did the bee say to the dirt-track rider?

Billy says,

No vaudeville now. No Brown Clown act, wasn't that it? No bad jokes, no curtain-lines, just plain drifting apart. I go my way, you go yours. And when you can see my way is my way, maybe we'll meet up again. O.K.?

Bumbo says,

I don't understand. After so long, I can't believe one. . . .

Billy says,

What's this one? Your Suffering Cerberus face? I've no sympathy left to spare. I'm weeping for myself, but you can't see it. The trouble with you, Bumbo, is that you're so bleeding versatile, you're such a bloody great Kohinoor with so many bloody great shining facets, you're so many things to so many people, that you've forgotten to get used to a face of your own. You're just a variety show. And it's a bad time for variety. Diminishing audiences. I'm the last one, and I've bought my last ticket. I tell you, you just don't know what anyone's like; they're just what you want to make them in the particular act you're playing. And I'm tired. And I'm bored. By god, I'm BORED. BORED. That's the one thing you said would end up any relationship of yours, to be told you're boring. Well, I think you're the biggest bore I wish I'd never met.

Bumbo says,

All right. If that's how you feel. If you feel better later on, I won't hold it against you.

Billy says,

Noble. Oh so noble. But it's how I do feel. And will continue to feel. So, do you mind, I'm tired. Bye, bye.

Billy lies back on the bed, his hands crossed behind the back of his head. Bumbo opens his mouth to speak, but all he can say is,

Bye.

He goes out of the room, closing the door. He walks down the stairs, and across the hall, past the couples amorously twining. From the corner of his eye, he sees his reflection in a window-pane, backed by the night outside. He turns to look at himself. At that moment, the light behind him is switched out, to shrieks and giggles and the clack of high heels running on stone. Bumbo, looking for his face, sees no face, but he hears the laughter all around him.

PART TWO

Bumbo in Season

So I wish you first a
Sense of theatre; only
Those who love illusion
     And know it will go far:
Otherwise we spend our
Lives in a confusion
Of what we say and do with
     Who we really are.

W. H. AUDEN: *From Collected Shorter
Poems* (1930–44)

4

BUMBO ON GUARD

Oh, it was the finest Battalion in London; and there were two. It contained the Commanding Officer, always called *Sir*; and Tibs, the Second-in-Command; and the Adjutant, Captain Bounois (nick-named Belleyes from the fascination of his glance), who wore the tightest and shiniest riding-boots Adjutant ever had, and got varicose veins. Then there were the majors, Farquhar the Laird, quiet Jinx, and Jorum, and the redoubtable Pigs, wounded and decorated in Viet-Nam, while on leave from dull jungle-fighting in Malaya. And then came the captains, Pegtop, Lickspittle and Pouf, immaculate trio of depressed discretion, Adjutants hoping-to-be. Five Lieutenants too, filthy Fred, Bouncer the Dwarf with his guardian Little (two hundred pounds, seventy-nine inches, three thousand a year); and Wills and Whiff, the unmentioned, living on their pay. Nine ensigns made up the Mess. Four there already, Fitz, Jujube and Mad Mike, who swung on the chandelier first night in Germany, and next morning was *en route* to Aldershot (P.T. Course); plus the soak, no-soda-please, Mack-Jones. The Young Ensigns filled up the quota, Laughing Gus (whom all loved), Maypole Bean,

Bumbo, proud Outram, and the Fly Crutcher, still on the make, and unmade. And the Captain (QM), called Sunny; ex-private, the best of them all.

R.S.M. Biggs led the Sergeants' Mess; when he took his belt off, his chest fell down to his belly. J. Brash was Drill-Sergeant with Gentleman Jim, smooth-voiced as a B.B.C. announcer. Then came the Sergeants and Lance-Sergeants, but their names need not be mentioned, except for those in the Rugby team. These were Sgt. Peters, L/Sgts. Johnson and James, P. And, in charge of the clothing-stores, the unctuous Quartermaster-Sergeant Issy.

Full Corporal was Cpl. James, A; with L/Cpls. Simons and Phillips, who threw six teddy-boys one night into the Serpentine. And L/Cpl. Thompson was Pay-Clerk, in charge of HQ Company documents.

There were also some four hundred Guardsmen. Four of them practised Rugby in the Park. Their names were Bart and Matt, and Gdsn. Thad the Lad. Gdsn. Andrewes too, the prop of the front row.

In case the Young Officers developed high-and-mighty ideas between their commissioning and their joining the Battalion at Wellington Barracks—affectionately called Welly B. by the cognoscenti—they were sent to the Adjutant on their arrival. He told them to give away their clothes to a ragman, and to get new clothes from certain specified tailors and hatters; then he put them straight on a month's drill course with a batch of young N.C.O.'s under the voice of Gentleman Jim. They were, perhaps, chased up and down more than at Caterham; they now wore swords which tripped them up as they marched; each performance ended ridiculously, when their tormentor formally saluted the Senior Young Ensign, and asked permission to dismiss the Squad. For they were now little scarlet gods, little bowler-hatted gentlemen. Bumbo, however, was so inefficient that he had to do two drill courses running; while waiting for an order, he always occupied his mind with some fascinating thought or another, so that, when the word of command came, he was invariably late, playing a virtuoso solo when harmony was expected.

Each Young Officer was given a private servant, to dress him in the armour of his divinity. The sole duty of this man was to bend his officer's cap with a wet towel, to brush his bowler, to spit on the pointed toes of his George boots, to polish his engraved sword, to wash his white gloves, and, before getting on parade, to brush the hair of his master's bearskin over his eyes, like a trainer pulling the fringe of the embroidered mat over the arse of a circus elephant. If an officer was improperly dressed on parade, Belleyes, the Adjutant, would never rebuke him, except at second-hand. Mr. Bailey, he would say, you will tell your servant to adjust your left trouser-leg one half of one inch downwards before you come on parade in the future.

The Young Ensigns were assigned to the various Companies. Bumbo was put in "B" Company, Farquhar's little lot. Farquhar was seventy-five inches of Scots Wha' Hae, all red face, righteousness, fair moustache, ladder-back, and a manner like thunderclouds in the sunset over the Orkneys; it wasn't that he was stupid, but nobody had ever managed to persuade him that he was wrong. For a month, he treated Bumbo like an untrained gundog, making him wipe up ten times over the non-existent messes he said Bumbo had made. Then he upgraded Bumbo to the rank of deferential subordinate and possible equal, off duty; but he made himself quite clear, that he did not like clever shits, so none of that stuff round *his* Company office.

Bumbo found a certain joy in the practice of the Battalion. The day was regularized. 0830 hrs, Company Orders. 0900 hrs, Drill Squad, in periods till lunchtime. 1400 hrs onwards, Company business, supervising the Platoons, until Farquhar was satisfied, or wanted to go home. Then, 1600 hrs or so, freedom, to wander out through London, or to take tea in the Barracks, bathe, and change for whatever function was going on that evening—(the Ensigns of the Brigade-of-Guards-Battalions-stationed-in-London were invited to most society dances, on the pre-National Service assumption that New Ensigns were lousy with money and background).

Occasionally, Bumbo was Picquet Officer, on duty in the Officers' Mess for twenty-four hours; then he was charged with overseeing the men's meals, inspecting the prisoners in the Guardroom, and checking the falling fabric of the Barracks, condemned fifty years back, but still inhabited. At least the façade was beautiful, at the side of Buckingham Palace, looking towards St. James's Park, over the railings of Birdcage Walk.

But the Ensign, who got most of a kick out of the life, was Mad Mike MacHaffie. His usual method of entering a room was at the run. He would seize the back of an armchair, and hurl himself over the top; his legs would travel in a full circle, like the arms of a windmill; he would end sitting on the noise of broken springs, and say, Where's the whisky?

He had a passion for shooting, and, on his first night in the Battalion, he was persuaded that the ducks in St. James's Park were reared as a special duck shoot for Brigade Officers stationed in Welly B. Dawn found Mike hidden behind a tree in the Park; and, as the tame ducks rose, "flighting", in the air, Mike began bringing them down. He was stopped by the keepers, after destroying several pintails, an asian guineascoot, and a lesser crested grebe.

At one period of his two years' National Service, Mike was wanted by the police in five countries, (the only five countries he had visited in Europe), for driving offences. The police could never find him; for the Officers' Mess barman had a standing order to state that Mr. MacHaffie was always Absent on Leave, which he frequently was, especially when there was a good race meeting on. The police did catch him once, in bed, in Pirbright Camp in Surrey. Are you Mr. MacHaffie?, said the Police-Sergeant. No, said Mad Mike, but I'll just go and get him. He walked out of the door, and disappeared.

He eventually left the thankful Army. Two years later, a constable stopped a Redston Officer for riding a bicycle without lights, at night, during a training scheme near Pirbright. The constable asked the

Officer for his name. The Officer answered, Smith-Aubyn. The policeman shone his torch in the Officer's face, looked at him, shook his head, and said,

Oh no, you're not, sir. Don't you lie to me. Your name is Mr. MacHaffie. All the crime in this district is done by Mr. MacHaffie.

At last, in May, Bumbo began Public Duties—the Bank Picquet, Tower Guard, Street lining, and Ensign of the Queen's Guard. The Bank Picquet would march off in the late afternoons, across the Horseguards Parade, down to the Embankment, along by Black-friars Bridge, up through the City into the great doors of the Bank of England. Bumbo led them, his jaw pressing against the chin-strap of his bearskin, to keep the seven-pound wicker-cage steady in the wind. He would feel his scarlet tunic stretching against the swing of his left arm, while he held his sword steady in his right hand, as a point of pride, all the way, four miles to the Bank. Occasionally, two weird middle-aged women would pace them, solemnly marching on the pavement beside them into the City. Nobody ever discovered who they were, or why they did it. They were christened Fortnum and Mason.

The fun of the Bank Picquet was that the Officer was ordered never to halt, not even for traffic jams and red lights. Bumbo would step along his appointed way boldly, secure in the knowledge that the rushing cars would skid to a stop about him. If the road was hope-lessly blocked, the Picquet mounted the pavement, three-abreast, while the pedestrians scattered. The

Reds, the vanguard of progress, could never mark time. It was said that, in the General Strike, the sight of the Bank Picquet marching to do their duty every day stiffened the morale of the brave bourgeoisie in their gallant resistance; and certainly the strikers never even booed them.

Of course, it took Mad Mike to lose his way, and march the Picquet round the wrong side of the river in a ten miles' detour. But even worse, one evening, he found an impassable traffic-jam and a blocked pavement. In a fit of inspired genius, he marched the whole Picquet down what he took to be the subway under the road. Tramp, tramp, tramp, in perfect threes, the Picquet entered a public lavatory. Mike unabashed, ripped open his fly-buttons, relieved himself, said, It happens to all of us, and marched them out again. The men loved him.

The Bank of England provided a private flat and dinner for the Officer of the Guard and one male guest; they also presented him with a free bottle of wine and port—sherry and whisky were thrown in for good measure. This was a relic of atavistic drinking-days. Bumbo once had a wooden-legged acquaintance in to dine; the man unstrapped his pin to drink the better; Bumbo had to support him, singing, past the sentries stationed along the corridors, and had to deposit him in the street, where he stood top-heavy, using his wooden stump as a walking-stick, while disapproving Bank officials looked severely at Bumbo, and spun shut the wheels of the steel outer door. Later, Bumbo always remembered the marches back, at six in the glooming mornings, with the murk rising off the

Thames, and a head on him like a gritty pint of bitter.

The Tower Guard was enjoyable for its forty-eight hours' comparative solitude—such a relief after the endless card-playing on Queen's Guard, where the four Guards officers made up a Bridge-hand, and it was difficult to cut out. Bumbo liked particularly the early morning rounds, between two and five, when black tongues of fog licked under the spikes of the Traitor's Gate, and the ravens croaked like damned souls, so that Bumbo swung round, slashing with his sword at nothing; and when, backed by a burly Sergeant, flanked by two Guardsmen, and led by a Drummer Boy holding a lantern, Bumbo gave the password to the yawning Yeoman Warder at the Inside Gate, so that he could open the door, and let the officer through, to inspect the Main Gate Sentry. Then there was the Ceremony of the Keys; the men drawn up on the sloping cobbles of the evening; the shouted order, GUARD AND ESCORT, PRESENT ARMS; the sword-hilt touched to his lips, and dropped sharp to the correct angle against his thigh; the bass-voiced warder, booming GOD PRESERVE QUEEN ELIZABETH; and they all say, AMEN, even Bumbo, while the trumpeter plays the Last Post, and it's all impossibly feudal and stupid and wunnerful and weepie, and somehow Bumbo can't mock. He even thinks of spending the night in the Tower Chapel, keeping vigil (in the manner of the Old Knights) where they laid the bodies of Lady Jane Grey and Bloody Mary; but he laughs at himself—better Captain Blood, trying to make off

68

with those impossible baubles, the Crown Jewels.

As for the Ensign of the Guard, it was a proud morning for the bhoy, to lift up that Colour so high, snide and handsome; and if there weren't two or three thousand Christopher Robins, Alices, Dollar Bills and Old Colonials watching the Changing of the Guard every time he did it. Full House for every performance. And, more satisfactory than applause, respect. Instead of laughter, awe. No boos and catcalls, but oohs and aahs. And the swing of the jerk-step of the slow march in the forecourt of the Palace, with the butt of the Colour sunk in its socket by his crutch, while the Brass Band slams out Figaro,

> *. . . Milanol . . . lol-lol-lol . . . lol-lol-LOLLO,*
> *By the left, by the right, by the CENTRE,*
> *Dee-dah-dah . . . dee-dah-dah . . . dee-dah-DADDA,*
> *By the right, by the left, by the FRONT. . . .*

And there was the occasional Street Lining, when the poor bastards of Guardsmen behind Bumbo had to stand still for five or six hours, spaced regularly as the girls along Curzon Street, while the Golden Coach rolled out and back again, and loyal populace huzzaad cheerfully. Bumbo, at least, could walk up and down, pretending to inspect his men; or, stood At Ease, he could rest his hands on his sword, its blade bent with its end jabbing the tarmac, as he leaned forward over his pointed toecaps, set the regulation eighteen inches apart.

Public Duties had their moments for Bumbo, but repetition bored him, and, after ten days a month On Guard for six months, he had had Public Duties. The only diversion was the visit of his Seasonal acquaintances, who came to see him in the Bank, or the Tower of London, or on Queen's Guard; but, as he seemed to know in London only the débutantes and their gay, young men, who bored him outside his Army Life, he was not amused by them on the inside. Moreover, drinks were expensive, and Bumbo, compared with his contemporaries, was poor. Thus he gave up inviting people to visit him. Later, Susie came sometimes, and Jock once. But that was all.

5

BEST BEHAVIOUR

Once the Season had started in May, the dances followed each other regularly and monotonously. Off Duty, Bumbo was too poor, and too bored, to stay and drink in the Barracks, when wine, what-passed-for-women, and Tommy Kinsman were offered him outside. He joined the rat-race of the Seasonal men, and strolled among the ragbags of puppy-fat and easy meat, that answered to the name of débutantes. He sunk his teeth in truffles and *foie gras*, and touched his lips to glasses and girls, who tasted impartially of champagne and Shocking Pink. Sure in the knowledge that he was one of a limited number of young men, qualified by postal address and education as escorts, he behaved as foully, stupidly, drunkenly, and rudely as the rest. He thought he knew that there were too many invitations and too few escorts, and that hospitality was, on the whole, unwilling—the good hosts were fools, and the bad, blackguards. In fact, the whole racket was a badly-organized, commercial marriage mart, screened by a venial veneer of ex-aristos.

It was true that some of his acquaintances did marry among the débutantes; but they married the parents, and took their bride along with a stack of solid Industrials. Yet marriages were few; the girls, although pleasant, were too young; most of them were barely eighteen, "finished" in Paris or Florence before their education had started. Only the really stupid City men would consent to appear more than two Seasons running; yet even morons would not pop the question, unless it was a question of money. Therefore the vacancies among the escorts were filled up, in the Eton holidays, among the ranks of the very young, who couldn't marry, and the Brigade of Guards, who wouldn't. Those men who were rich and eligible did not choose teen-agers as their wives. The Season was purposeless. But some found it enjoyable.

Bumbo always thought the whole brouhaha was such an odd way of having fun. Clemençeau had once said of the English dancing, *Ah, les anglais, avec le visage si triste, et le derrière si gai*; but Bumbo, looking round the room at one of the hops in Claridge's, could not see any pair of buttocks that seemed to be enjoying themselves.

The most miserable of all there were those female duets or trios of ugly sweet-seventeens, who stood talking brightly to each other, desperately not noticing that they were not being noticed. Every dance of the sixty in the Season was torture to them; convention demanded that they could not take their lonely taxi home until at least one o'clock in the morning; and, to justify all the expense, they had to appear to be happy, although Bumbo thought that their parents should be prosecuted by the R.S.P.C.A. for deliberate and pro-tracted cruelty to pets. Meanwhile, they stood, in

72

their giggles and gaggles, with their chaste cheeks behind and before tight with the effort of not seeming abandoned. Their eyes, seeking rescue, seeking any old family joke so long as he wore trousers, twitched ceaselessly away from each other round the noisy room, while their lips continued to open and shut, as they let out the conventional adjectives of enjoyment. If a wandering male, met once six months ago, came within five yards of a deserted group, he would be hailed by the castaways as though he were the Admiral of the Home Fleet; if he was green to the game, or moved by compassion, they would suck him into the puddle of their gossip, until he felt a moral obligation to save one of the girls by asking her to dance, anything for partial escape. If, however, he was an old hand at the game, and beyond pity, he would drop his excuses in their laps like a visiting-card, promising to come back later, after a brief call on a waiting partner, a long-unseen friend, or the cloakroom. Bumbo usually carried two full drink-glasses in his hand, so that his excuse for passing on, that he was taking some champagne to another girl, always seemed reasonable. Anyway, he could drink twice as much. But once, caught without glasses, he had had to plead claustrophobia; the girl had offered to accompany him outside to the fresh air; eventually, Bumbo had gone back to the Barracks early in full retreat, although he had been enjoying himself and had wanted to stay.

Bumbo looked round the room to pick out some of his more flattering acquaintances, notably those few who came from that unhappy portion of the inbred offspring of the continental millionaires, who thought it *très snob* to bring out their young in the last society in Europe with most of the nineteenth-century trappings and a few sixteenth-century titles.

After Bumbo had made his funnies *en passant* to those who would be useful in the future, he looked out his three favourite gay girls, who prettily passed the time doing nothing in particular but doing it very well; dark-haired Jojo, skipping about like a lotus-lily, agitated by a bee; Loo, smiling her sidelong mouth at him in an invitation to come along and have a good sit-down later; and Susanna, who had slapped his face once, for no other reason than that she felt like warming her cold hands. But they were all attached to limpets of partners, three *vacua*, who seemed to Bumbo worse off than the Three Fates; certainly they could see, and perhaps they had their own teeth, but they only shared, as a trio, one back to their heads and half a chin.

Sheila was there, gay as confetti. She patronized Bumbo now, when she saw him, saying, God, how *young* we were then. But she seemed to like him. This time she did not see him. She was clasped in standing, shut-eyed ecstasy round a tall axe-faced boy from Oxford. She was saying, *Please. Pretty please.*

Yet Bumbo was even more puzzled by the sexual ethics of the socialites, than he was by the fun they said they got out of large social occasions. The débutantes went in big for what the Americans call "heavy petting" and the euphemistic English "working arrangements". There wasn't all that much sleeping around, unless some particular Season thought sleeping fashionable rather than pleasurable; good for curiosity and keeping up with the Smyth-Browne-Joneses rather than good for nature and keeping up with D. H. Lawrence.

For the social men, although left completely in control by the post-war breakdown of the chaperone system, managed quite successfully to divorce love and sex from each other. The first was for the blue-blooded amateurs, whom they might marry; the second was for the professionals, whose function it was. They adapted a popular song to demonstrate the point.

> *Love and sleeping, love and sleeping,*
> *The one's for keeps, and the other's for keeping,*
>> *You can have one,*
>> *Yes, you can have one,*
>> *You can have one without the other.*

Bumbo himself would have thought it less immoral if the men had slept with the girls they professed to love, and had given the professionals a miss. But he, in turn, was accused of immoralism. What if it were *your* daughter? Good luck to her, said Bumbo, as long as they really love each other, and her lover can afford to pay, if necessary, for those extended stays in appendix wards, or long vacations in Switzerland. For, in his romanticism, Bumbo still believed in one all-inclusive love, in which bed, brains, beauty and even boredom would all mix more smoothly than any Martini into an endless inebriation.

So the Season glimmered on through Ascot to Lords, until it bobbed out on the waves at Cowes. It was all so extravagant, so determinedly gay, so futile, so-so. Yet Bumbo, flattered by his semi-success in a new environment, where masks were requested and men were clothes-hangers, quite enjoyed his experiences. And if his later meeting with Jock and Susie taught him to find the conversation of the socialites inane, their emotions childish, their sense of values pernicious, and their very existence intolerable, yet, for a little while, he was flattered, Bumbo from suburbia, at being accepted as one of them; and he was prepared to excuse them, in gratitude for their mistaken favours.

6

SOLO FOR AN ENSIGN

Bumbo was made Rugby Officer, because he said he didn't mind, and all the others did. The Fly Crutcher had naturally fixed himself as Gardening Officer, since there was only tarmac in Wellington Barracks. Poor Laughing Gus confessed in a weak moment, that, though he liked drinking, he thought water was poison; they made him Swimming Officer.

The Rugby team used to practise during some afternoons in Hyde Park; once a week they used to take a truck to a ground in the suburbs, to play other Army teams. They played Rugby Union; although the men were all northerners and preferred Rugby League.

Bumbo enjoyed these games, and mocked at himself for enjoying them. He played full back or wing forward; sometimes the men would forget Bumbo was not one of them, and they would shout, curse and swear at him. Even off the field, on the long journey home in the box-back of the three-ton truck, they seemed to like him. Physically tired and easy-feeling, Bumbo laughed with them; he found them bawdy and funny, without wit or sneer; men who loved laughter for the good feeling it gave, like brown ale, in their stomachs. And, when they arrived back too late for

77

normal dinner, Bumbo, in the regulation manner, would see that they ate, before he ate himself. He would wander round the cookhouse, watching them bolt their wads of bread and fishcakes, smothered in ketchup; they would wash down the mixture with the brown syrup they called tea, that lined their bowels as comfortingly as lime lines a kettle.

Bumbo, since he was the only officer, was automatically Captain of the team, although in fact Sergeant Peters picked the side, and gave the list to Bumbo for formal approval. But, during the game, Bumbo would shout and plead, as he broke away from the scrums, dribbling the ball at his feet, After me, Reds. Follow me. Come after me. We're going to win.

And they did follow him.

Yet Bumbo was never sure whether they really accepted him, until the day when he was Picquet Officer On Duty, and Sergeant Peters marched in to see him, saying that he was wanted by the prisoner in the Guardroom.

Who is it?, Bumbo says.

It's Guardsman Smiley, sir. "A" Company.

But he didn't have any complaints when I did my rounds this morning.

He hasn't got any complaints. He just wants to see you, sir. He says it's a private matter, sir.

But I'm not his Platoon Officer, nor his Company Commander. It wouldn't be regular. Why does he want to see *me*, and not *them*?

Sergeant Peters lowers his voice confidentially, You're the only officer in the Barracks, sir.

And besides, he says he's scared of officers. But he'll see *you*, sir.

Bumbo went to see him. This was the measure of Bumbo's success and failure in the Redston Guards. He was still a person, not an officer; still human, not divine; still as the other men were, not only as his own sort were. He was guilty of humanity, condemned for being familiar.

Guardsman Smiley sprang up, quick as a down-bent sapling, when Bumbo in his Blues came into the room, the gold-braided peak of his cap pulled down over his eyes, his ebony Picquet-cane tucked with its silver-balled head behind his armpit.

Well, Bumbo says, what is it, Smiley?

Smiley stutters,

It's my girl, sir. Let me out, sir, and I swear to God I'll be back in twenty-four hours, but I've got to marry her, sir, or she won't half catch it home.

Bumbo says,

What exactly is the case?

Sergeant Peters interposes,

Well, sir, this morning a young . . . *lady* was reported by the sentry at the gate, as trying to hold converse with him. On duty, sir. So I tells the young *lady* to desist. So she goes away. I didn't think it was worth my while bothering you, sir, seeing as how officers don't like being bothered, and since this sort happens every day. But this one comes back, and informs me that she will have words with the prisoner, she will. And she'll stay until she does, 'cos she hasn't got any money to get back home with. So I go and see the prisoner, and he asks me to see you, sir. That's how it is, sir.

Bumbo says,

Where is she now?

Sergeant Peters says,

She's still outside the railings, sir.

Bumbo says,

March her in, Sarnt Peters.

Sergeant Peters comes back in a few minutes with a white-faced girl in a raincoat. She is five or six months' pregnant. She is frightened. She looks quickly at the prisoner, bites her lips, and tries to stand to attention like him.

Bumbo says, embarrassed,

Please sit down, won't you?

Thank you, sir, says the girl, and remains standing.

Bumbo says,

Look, I'm here to help you. If there's anything I can do, I'll do it.

Oh, sir, she says, just let him out, so as he can marry me, and I swear I'll bring him back myself, honest to God, we can get it all over and done in a day, it's all fixed, and I swear honest I won't keep him, and you must believe me, sir.

She cries. Bumbo tells the prisoner to stop standing to bloody attention, and go and stop her crying. They sit side by side on the stripped bed-frame, swearing to God, on their honour, cross their heart, that all will be rosy and hunky-dory, if only the prisoner can have twenty-four hours, to do right by the girl he has wronged.

All right, says Bumbo.

He finds out that the man has another fortnight to spend in the Guardroom, that he has been there a week. It is impossible to get hold of the Commanding Officer on the telephone to regularize the release of the prisoner. Bumbo decides to carry the can himself.

The prisoner's pay has been stopped, so Bumbo lends him five pounds. Bumbo explains that *he* will be punished if the prisoner does not return, and that he is only allowing the prisoner Absence of Leave because he trusts him. The prisoner and the girl, who says she is called Mary, start up their chorus of gratitude and promises again. Bumbo cuts them short, and returns to the Officers' Mess. Sergeant Peters sniffs, and sets the prisoner free.

Naturally the prisoner does not return. Although he does marry the girl, it is not even his baby, apparently. And he remains on the run for three months. Bumbo is reprimanded by the Commanding Officer for stupidity, and given a week's extra Picquet Duty.

You bloody fool, Farquhar says, why didn't you leave it till the morning, when the whole thing could have been dealt with properly? That girl would have found somewhere to sleep, I bet you. All that sort always do. In the Brigade, boy, you do as the Brigade says.

And when our sort, Bumbo says, have a little slip-up, oh, we can always pay for the abortion, can't we? Or marry them, because we don't get put in jail. Tell me, Farquhar, is it never right to side-step Standing Orders? Maybe, you know, the Brigade is made for man, not man for the Brigade.

Don't be so bloody smart, blast you, Farquhar shouts. Too many brains always gets you into trouble. You don't go around being a bloody Samaritan here; you look it up in Standing Orders. And ten to one Standing Orders is right. I tell you because I know.

Farquhar, as usual, was correct. Bumbo knew it, but he had to say, I might have been right.

But you weren't, were you, Farquhar says. Just show me once you are right, and the Brigade's wrong, and I'll eat my bloody bearskin.

Bumbo is stubborn.

Look, he says, maybe I was wrong this time, and I was proved wrong, but I might have been just a bit right. You go on being just a bit right a lot of times, and it's all right in the end.

Stop muddling me, Farquhar says, and do as you're told. How do think we'd run the ruddy Brigade if every twopenny-ha'penny Ensign thought he could do as he liked. You can't run any unit in the Army unless you do as you're told.

Why is a division called a division?, Bumbo says innocently.

Because it's divided . . . oh, no, it's not, Farquhar roars. Stop tripping me up, you clever shit. Just get on with the job you're told to do, and stop being so bloody conceited. Fall out.

Bumbo fell out with most of the Officers' Mess. Overtly, they were all on the best of terms with him. It was the convention that even rage should be expressed like an invitation to dinner; for only Bumbo became warmly angry, while the others were merely "not amused", and said so. Yes, they used swear-words, it was true; but meaninglessly, to show that they were military men. Officers, to be gentlemen, wore stars on their shoulder straps, and said shit. Expletives were not explosives, but rusty shell-cases, to be dumped up and down military training areas, so that normal people could know that Army had passed, and was passing. Swearing was, for Redsmen, a habit, and thus had no effect upon them; anger then, to be effective, had to be controlled. And Bumbo, speaking up for strikers, oppressed races, and art, and other leftish rag, tag and bobtail, was too vehement to make any impression. To the Redston officers, a man who said strongly what he meant was either foolish (and they thought Bumbo clever), drunk (and Bumbo was usually sober), or wrong (and Bumbo was far too eccentric to be right). Only Laughing Gus used to speak on Bumbo's side, saying that even if Bumbo wanted the trees to walk topsy-turvy with their roots in the air, maybe he was right, and the world would be a better place if everyone stood on their heads to look round. Like a Yogi.

But Bumbo could not even *seem* honest about his family. His father, proud as a rooster about his commission, agreed to give Bumbo an allowance of two hundred and fifty pounds a year, over and above his pay. He could not afford this much, but Bumbo painted such a despairing scene of moneyless Guardees in the gay city, that his father was persuaded. Yet Bumbo, when asked for his home address by the Battalion, gave a false one, that of Maypole Bean's flat, where he sometimes slept the night. And he told his parents never to telephone him at the Barracks, except in cases of extreme urgency. To his brother officers, he hinted darkly of recent bereavement, and managed to flush, when he was asked about his parents—the questioners always took this redness for grief, not guilt, and delicately changed the subject. It was not, Bumbo rationalized to himself, that he was ashamed of his background and suburban address; but it was really too much of a bore to explain continually in a snob-society that he had nothing in common with his family, and that he was far more the product of Eton and the Brigade than of Penge and Potter's Bar.

As the days on parade succeeded the days on parade, and the Season (that was the only season of the year) grew middling, Bumbo felt routine sitting like a handle on the ramrod of his back. His mind seemed to be shrivelling up inside his skull, as a bad walnut in its shell. All idea of himself as the recorder of human folly, the Tolstoy of the febrile fifties, the saviour of future degenerations, had left Bumbo. Even his anger at the sameness of the Brigade had turned into acceptance and despair. Granted the need of last ditchers, death and glory boys, and ceremonial mannequins, the Brigade fulfilled its functions admirably. It had endured for three hundred years, and was still enduring and endured. Bumbo was merely the umpteenth Young Ensign, whose job was to make the perfect perfection, by the meticulous application of the rules. If equipment did not fit a man, it was the man who was warped. Guardsmen *were* made for the Brigade, not the Brigade for Guardsmen. Bumbo's job was to pick fluff off the soldiers' tunics, and to drop it on the floor; then he could swear at them for leaving fluff on the floor.

He had to make them brush their bearskins, until the fringe of hair hung down enough to blind them; then he could curse them for saying that they did not see. For Bumbo knew that soldiers should not be able to see, and that officers should wear blinkers, so their course might be set everlastingly by Standing Orders, and by the example of the Majors who had been Ensigns below Majors who had also been Ensigns, etcetera, etcetera, etcetera, for ten generations, since The Reds saved the Crown of England. Bumbo reckoned that if the Devil had been a Redsman, Hell would be a Guardsman's Heaven, of shouts and commands and lunacy by numbers, with the imps in threes Presenting (human) Arms for their Commanding Officer's inspection.

There was no possibility of unfairness in the Brigade, since Standing Orders were more applicable to every daily situation than any Bible. All punishment was foreseen and limited; no Job could complain of unjust persecution. For where Standing Orders did not apply, manners did. God may propose, but good taste disposes. Discontent may be divine, but conventions are human. Outward conformity was all that the Brigade demanded. As long as an officer wore a bowler-hat, it would be a sufficient cover for any rebellious skull. But the bowler-hat must always be worn; there was no relief from duty. The whole Redsman was expected to be the whole Redsman, integrated, discreet, correct for twenty-four hours in every day. Bumbo even thought it was safer to sleep with his mouth shut.

7

EXISTENCE EXPRESSO

Bumbo, finding Life neither in the Brigade nor in the Season, went to Chelsea to look for it.

In the first Expresso bar, no one talked to him. In the second, a middle-aged man put a fond hand on his knee, which made Bumbo rise sharply, saying, Sorry, I must go now, and meet my girl-friend.

Girl-friend, girl-friend, said the middle-aged man, don't say those horrible words. Say sister.

Well, she's a sister to me, said Bumbo, and left on the curtain-line, unfortunately forgetting his overcoat, so that he had to go back and retrieve it, apologetically.

But, in the third Expresso bar, sat Jock, balancing his body on the high bar-stool, like an egg on a sherry-glass. He was all mobile mouth and cardigan-wrapped abdomen, on which his hands rested folded, as though on a table. His face was the face of the podgy dough-men little children make from cake-mix scrapings, but, instead of currants, he had blackening cocktail-cherries for eyes. His mouth was changing shapes, slithering the one into the other, as he talked.

. . . When Jock's in his coffee-bar, all's wrong with the world. Ah, look at that bit of all right, just flew in from Mamma's. New spaces, new faces, new embraces . . . come into my arms, my beamish boy. No. I'm not one of *those*; I just know what I like, and I like you, you walking streak of class-prejudice. Sit you down, and tell Nunky Jock, hoo's tha' auld City wurrrld bin mollockin' ye around the noo? Any more Bank leaks lately, or has the Thames run dry? . . .

Bumbo says,

I'm not a City man.

. . . No, you're a broth of a boyo, really. It's just the miscut of your jibbooms and bob-stays. I shouldn't have made the bloomer, you've got an honest face. So you'd better look at me with the back of your head. No, no, no. Second thoughts. I'd rather see the front of you; I can't stand all that neat horticulture on the back of your neck. It takes me back to those old suburban gardens, in Maida Vale, and Pinner; you've got every blade of hair mowed into place, and there's the faint odour of Honey-and-Flowers. You'll catch your death of bees, I shouldn't wonder. . . .

The bar boys-and-girls laughed. Bumbo smiled self-consciously.

. . . Is that a smile that I see before me? It looked to me very-U, mind you, but a U the wrong-way round. Equals n. Do you always keep a down-turned horseshoe in your mouth? No, don't listen to me, really. I'm a sucker for the gentry; you'll always find me semi-attached. You're all such good listeners. That's the nice things about people with manners . . . they let you hear yourself talk. And I like that. Hey, what's your name? . . .

87

I'm called Bumbo, said Bumbo.

  . . . I like that too. Don't tell me you've got a sense of humour. . . .

  I have laughed once or twice, Bumbo said.

  . . . Goodie, goodie peppermints. Hey, let's just us go to Babylon—that's what I call my place. You, know, how many miles to Babylon; just five minutes walk, duckie, and keep those candles for where the good Lord made a place for them. There'll be a party going on at home; there always is. Since my old mum left me a million, there's always been a party there, my friends being what they is. I don't go there much now, myself; there's no place like abroad. But I want you to try my special cocktail—it's called a brain-washer—I got it off an old Freud of a psycho-analyst, who always used to say, In Vodka Veritas. But you can have too much of that Russian lark, what I say is, Don't be so bloody, Mary, let's be normal some of the month. . . .

During this overflow of sounds, Jock had put on his coat, paid his bill, and whisked Bumbo out into the street. They were walking along the King's Road.

  Bumbo said,

  Look, I've got to be on early parade to-morrow, so make it quick and short.

  . . . Oh, you're one of them, eh—the Gay Guardees, seeing how the people live, and living like some of the people. . . . We really are one of *you*, chaps; we like sex, slumming, and cool jazz too. As Humph said at the Chelsea Palace, a cat can look at a Queen. But don't you worry, Bumboboy, I know a fellow soul when I see one. No codpiece, honest. You

88

just try it out for size *chez moi*, and if you like it, the door is always wide-open, for you to get kicked out of. You're welcome on the mat. This is Liberty Hall, and by liberty I mean unlicensed, drink on the house, guaranteed Sanforized against head-shrinking. Sorry, I talk too much. And I really want to talk about you. Tell me all, background, behaviour-patterns, and breeding, do you like it, and if so, why? Jockey-boy, get out of the saddle, and give your friend a free rein, and that doesn't mean I want a bloody Hailsham. Oh, here we are, so you'll have to talk after. God, what a hellish noise, but this is home sweet home. . . .

So Jock's spiel babbled on to Babylon, a house near The Vale, luckily detached. And, in the following months, Bumbo came to love his talking stream, skirting pebbles, sliding past rocks, warm, reasonable, oh so reasonable, giggling in gutters, glancing away from the sun, mocking, punning, chuckling over the shallows, irritable in eddies, in irreverent whirlpools, and spilling away into irrelevant puddles. When Jock chose to damn the flood, Bumbo found himself chaffing back, chattering, confiding; he was drawn out of his imposed withdrawing, since Billy's going. Jock became his familiar spirit, his sainted Satan. And every evening that he was free, he would go to the house by The Vale.

Every one in Chelsea ended up *chez* Jock on some drunk or another. There were the characters, Holy Joe, Pegfoot, and the Adman, tattooed from navel to chin in Schweppes and Guinness signs, who, when lit-up, stripped off his shirt, rolled his muscles, and made Piccadilly Circus look like the blackout.

Scaggioni used to drop in from the Roma-Flight; and Paris Max; sometimes Da Rimini, still poor, though he was now in the American oil-widow trade.

And, of course, Agnelli was a regular. He was just abnormal. Instead of painting girls with pinheads and triangular thighs, as the good Picasso had made them, he improved on nature, and painted them as he thought they ought to be. His so-called art was strictly non-representational; it looked like an election in a totalitarian state, with only one candidate. For Agnelli always painted the same picture, that of a beautiful, curvular, cats-eyed, half-draped brunette, called Giovanna. Nobody had ever seen her, even Agnelli, except in his imagination. But, as he explained, every woman, every man, everything he saw looked like Giovanna. If he painted a house on canvas, it was Giovanna; a cow looked like Giovanna; so did a concrete-mixer, a self-portrait, a rubbish-dump. It wasn't that he couldn't draw anything else; of course not; it was just the way that his true artist's eye interpreted its surroundings. Even the ugliest hag who paid dearly, and sat for him, was transformed into a radiant beauty. So commissions poured in on the grateful Italian. Giovanna's face hung in every drawing-room in the country, with suitable titles underneath, such as "Sunset Over Taormina" or "The Last Comrade" or, quite simply, "Portrait of—" (a blank space was left for the buyer to fill in, at will, after purchase; somehow Agnelli seemed to know by instinct that every sitter would look just like Giovanna). The other painters thought Agnelli a fraud as a painter, but at least he was an honest business-man. He would shrug his shoulders, and say, Well, I spoil a clean canvas, my old mother milks a goat. I get ten pounds a minute, she won't sell anything. I drink my whisky, she drinks her milk. I get ulcers, she gets fat. Who wins on the deal?

Often Justin was in Jock's place, Justin, from the colonnaded house round the corner. He came with his husband, Knut, a terrible Swede. But they had been happily married for twenty years, and now, in their middle-age, had set up a *ménage à trois*, with the new singer from Trinidad, Harry Hardrada. They used to gossip with the other threesome, Molly (who didn't), Jane (who would no longer), and fair Jacqueline (who would still, but nobody wanted her).

In I.T.V. were Box, Chris, Della Piera, Frank, John (three times over), Matt, Patt, Rog and weary William; they brought with them their *models*, chick-and-pixie alike, the long and the short of it, skirted and flirting, suited and cute, bobbed, clipped, hipped, pipped on the post, lost and longing, lounging around, just resting, in slacks and casuals, exclusive-bargain, cut-price, cash on delivery, or any old how. An old painter sometimes doddered round, while heavy blondes tickled him, and begged for a picture to sell to the galleries. And, in the corner, a committed trio committed themselves angrily, in high-pitched voices, saying, Potts, Potts, that's not the name for a genius, nor is Smithson, nor Richards, but we are the only three genii living.

Bumbo thought this was Life.

Then, one evening, Black Juju blew in from the

Bahamas, and tinkled the lyrics of "Shed Me, Fred",
now in its third year in New York,

> *My last one said, I love you, Fred,*
> *Darling, I know that I should,*
> *But I like a man, who really can,*
> *Never a man who could,*
> > *I heard her laughter as I went away*
> > *To learn that pretty game that one can play. . . .*

By the suggestive piano, humming, her arms hug-
ging her knees, sat a red-haired model-girl. She
didn't seem to notice any one there. She rocked
slightly to the rhythm. She wore a blue-and-white
striped singlet, and a grey skirt. Her body was beautiful. Her face changed like a chameleon from the pert,
to the pleasing, to the pleasurable, to the present face
to exclude all other faces. She had come with one of
the Johns; she had not spoken to him since she came;
when Bumbo asked her to dance, she looked at him
warily. She called up to Jock, who was standing
nearby.

What about *him*, Jockey?

Jock said, smiling.

Watch your two-step, duckie, he's the
wickedest man in the room.

After that introduction, Bumbo found it easy.
They went straight into a hard, standing clinch, sway-
ing vaguely to the beat of the piano; Bumbo could feel
her stomach-muscles rolling against the bone of his
hip, her finger-tips digging into the nerves of his
upper-arms. He felt sick, and hard; he closed his eyes;
he trembled. The music stopped. They sat down.

Yes, said Bumbo, yes.

She nodded.

For the rest of that evening, the masks shifted and slipped over Bumbo as he drank; the Sheik hinted, Buffo buffooned, Thistlethought teased, and the Beater, oh the Beater was sincere. Only Cerberus lay doggo, suffering in silence.

He took Susie, that was her name, home. And, standing on the doorstep below the flat where she lived alone, he said, shivering,

I don't know much, really.

Susie sucked him into the quicksand of her mouth,

Nor me, she said. Let's learn.

8

LOVERS

Yes, it was madsummer, three months Bedlam of lovers. Walking down the King's Road, buying shocking-pink Italian blouses; trumpets sounding for them as they ate hot dogs at Harringay, and the bowler-hatted kennel-girls led the greyhounds round the dirt-ring of the green oval, and waited patiently, while the exhibitionist-dog relieved itself, slowly, disdainfully, for the particular benefit of the man with brush-and-pan behind; lights lying like scythed grass in a wind on Thames-water, near Chelsea Bridge, by Flood Street; Susie, trying on his bearskin in the Tower, a black fur-cloud that giggled and shook on the white spurs of the hills of her shoulders; or dawdling, his arm round her waist, and his hand on her hip-bone, that rolled with her moving thigh under the thin skin of her trousers; kissing on benches, under streetlights, in jazz-clubs, on Guard, softly, with passion, in play, for the hell of it; leaving bowler-hats and umbrellas with friendly night-porters, ripping off stiff-collars and striped ties to keep tucked away in the pocket, hiding from khaki uniforms, as if they were the particular demons in a whole world of intruders; lying in the drowse of the heath beyond Putney, her head on his shirt, or else in her room, looking at the peeling grey-white of the ceiling, that hovered like cumulus to confine their love; laughing, shouting, staring, miming, in dialect, French, Yank, or spaghetti-Italian; but always, in everything, as one, meaning it.

Susie was an only child, an orphan. Like Bumbo, she preferred isolation, and living alone; but, she said, living with Bumbo was like living alone, they were so much together. She had had one or two brief lovers before; but she had never enjoyed it. This she told Bumbo, for they had sworn honesty, and they tried not to break the oath.

In the evenings, Susie would take off her clothes, her royal-blue shirt and blue trousers and black under-clothes, and they would get into bed together, and move in the strength and the pull of their bodies, bruising and biting each other. Yet, from time to time, Susie seemed so indifferent to what was the glory for Bumbo, that he hesitated, lost the moment, and lay, holding her, quivering, saying, Oh God, darling, I love you too much, too much, for it to be now. You must understand, darling. And Susie said, I do. And Bumbo knew that, when they could go away together, there would always be the glory; for glory was a habit, not a surprise.

They used to lie there, softly caressing, and talk, talk, always of themselves, until Susie would say, I've a big day tomorrow. You must go, darling. And Bumbo would reach out his hand, and turn on the reading-lamp, and pull back the sheet. And then he would say, Susie, you are beautiful. And she would say, Yes. Quite simply, for she was. And she knew, and

95

he knew, and they marvelled that they were them. Oh, the luck of it, and the chance of it, that they were each who they were, and that they were together. And Bumbo would kiss her. From her toes, that were the only ugliness in the supple and the spring of her body, he would run his lips, light as a shiver, along the white sprawl of her beauty, resting his head on the softness that was hard of her belly, then touching the points of her ribs, curving downwards, before he pushed with his hands the soft splay of her breasts into the hollows of his eyes, so that he was blinded with the full of the feel of the warm dark that was his love. Then with his mouth he would press her throat, under the jaw-bone, until she pulled away, gasping, and wound her hands in his hair, and laughed, and pouted her lips on his, sucking the breath from him, saying, Gosh, do you want to murder me? And Bumbo would say, Yes. And he would stand up beside her on the floor, and look once more at the long-lying length of her, and cover her with the sheet, tucking it in beneath the mattress. And he would bend, and touch with his tongue the hollow, the height of a fingernail above her eyebrows, the hub from where the lines of her face spoked out like on the surface of a sun-dial, to make the mask without a shadow, that said her name was Susie.

He would dress, and leave her sleeping. And, gradually, the whole series of actions became a ritual, a ceremonial, the bedding of Susie, to be played to a background of Radio Luxembourg, and yawns. For Susie lived in the moment. She was like an animal, rarely wanting to mate, who ate when she was hungry, drank when she was thirsty, and slept when she was tired. And she was more and more tired, every time that he saw her, for her modelling (helped by Bumbo's advice) became increasingly successful. And each night she went out with some necessary celebrity or other. Her room became full of toy-poodles that rich men bought her in night-clubs; but the rich men were stupid, and she had got a First at Reading University; and she hugged the poodles, and Bumbo, and said that they were all she loved. She told her other men about Bumbo, she said, and if they wanted to waste their money on her, well, a girl must eat. And Bumbo felt proud to hold her against this competition.

But somehow the time never came when they could go away together. When Bumbo's leave came, Susie was working. So Bumbo went off with Outram, to stay at Dinkley, and shoot at the hand-fed grouse, cosseted careful as babies. And, on his return, suddenly Susie wanted him desperately. And, until dawn, they fought, twisting and straining, tearing scratches down the oiled ropes writhing beneath the skins of their backs, with both voices crying, darling, oh my darling, for ever and ever my darling, god, god, for ever break on the grip of the arms, leg-lock, bite of the teeth on the moan.

Bumbo walked back to the Barracks in the dawn of that morning. Slight cold. Blue-metal sky. A water-cart dribbling and brush-whirling the streets. The edge of the houses with an outline sharp as a cheese-cutter. Bumbo felt peace bubble and burst within him, and pop in the gas-balloon of his head, until he had to force down his hips with his hands to keep himself on the pavement. Once in the Officers' Mess, he sat at a writing-desk, a glass of orange-juice beside him, occasionally glancing at the sentry on his beat, regular as a metronome, while Bumbo made words jig, fall, dance, rise and lie to the music of his love.

The paper was headed with the Brigade Star, and the legend,

4th Bn Redston Gds
Wellington Barracks
S.W.1.

My utter darling (Bumbo wrote),

I walked back from your room, and I knew that I was velvet, strung between two posts—blue velvet, that blue your breasts are under your shirt, that blue that is the weir that roars and slips away, shadowed by the saplings of your legs—I was blue velvet, strung between two posts, in a mill-race of blood, that bubbled and hammered, passed me, furied and flurried, and flicked me away, over and overturning, between the overhung arches of my ribs. And then the sun came, and shone upon me, coldly, and spread me out, warming me, until the blue cloth of me covered all the surface of the clotted water, and spilled over into the streets and the gardens, and the basements with the cats asleep in them, until as far as the eye of god above me could see, one huge joy of blue covered the earth and the sea and rose up beyond the horizon, and all that blue was me. And the sparrows sang me, and the blackbirds feathered me, and the sun came out on sympathy-strike for me, and people pointed to me, and said—look at the whole of one man's love, how it covers the world like a blanket, just the love of one small man, how it covers the world like a carpet, how it rises in its dream in the blue fog of the morning, and burns in the blue flame of the hills of Florence-noon, and sleeps in the blue shade of gentians and afternoon-trees, and stretches the evening across the field under the strength of its arms. Just the love of one man can fill the world? Who can be his love, that it should spill over so, and put a cloth round the globe? But they cannot know, and no one can know, who is not I; for my love is my love is my love, it is of me, for me, from me, to me, and I give it all to you, for my world is yours, and my world is the whole world is the world of you. . . .

Bumbo stopped writing to read the letter through. It was a good letter. The words said what he hadn't seen, but what he should have seen. He loved the love he manufactured for his love; manufactured love felt better, read better than actual love. For his actual love was for a series of trivialities, in the same way as the worst pain is often felt for something stupid like toothache.

Bumbo wrote again.

. . . . For one moment, the black-backed bitterness sat on my head like a cap on the wig of a murder judge, because I had to leave you. But then I lifted my hand to my head, and put the black cap aside. Prisoner at the bar of my love, I said, Guilty. I sentence you to hang on my neck until you are dead. Darling, we'll take that big drop again together, soonest. But, god,

Susie, *que je t'aime. Tout passe*, perhaps even us; but for the vision of my love covering the world that is you, for the seeing of the blue, that is me-and-you-and-you-and-me spread over all we know and are and will be, for this glance at nothing and everything, sometime-thing and utterthing, my darling, I thank you and I love you

Bumbo

Bumbo reread, put in some commas, addressed the envelope, placed the letter inside, stuck down the flap, and went to bed. It *was* so good, he thought. So phoney and so good. So like what it ought to have been that perhaps it was. Hell, what was memory to a man anyway, except to make him believe his make-believe?

9

A BREAK FOR BUMBO

With the sudden nationalization of the Suez Canal by the Egyptians, the concentration of British troops in Cyprus, and the call-up of the Home Reservists, Bumbo visited the Victoria and Albert Museum, to consider his course of action if the Battalion were ordered overseas. He wandered among the trophies of Empire, the spoils of India for the toils of Britain, no exploitation without some civilization, and could not decide on mutiny.

He went to a nearby coffee-bar to think, but he only managed to increase his indecision. He wanted to talk things out. Susie was away, so he telephoned Jock, asking him to come to the coffee-bar. On his arrival, Bumbo gave him a long harangue, joking but meaning it, about conscience, duty and the etceteras of personal responsibility. Jock put a finger alongside his nose, blew at the surface of his coffee, and, every twenty seconds or so, he shot quick sparks of glances from his red eyes at Bumbo. He says,

. . . You shake me, boyo. You look ten years older than your nice nineteen; why not act like it? Who do you think you are, the Messiah or something? Look, kid, you try to play the Christ, and you won't even be able to play the Devil. You'll just be playing for a low laugh in an empty house. There's no room left for saviours these days. Let's just have some down-to-earth men for a change, shall we? No more heroes, Bumbo, they're on the shelf, in the nursery with Winnie the Pooh and the Beatrix Potters. Just want what you can get. And if you get something you think you don't want, it's your thought that's wrong, not the thing. If you like all you're given by the whole lousy set-up, you're laughing, aren't you? Dead simple. No problems. . . .

Bumbo interrupts,

You're so bloody reasonable, Jockey. But you play it on the markets with a million. How would you do, if you were me?

Jock says,

Don't ask me for moral advice, buster; my essence is moist, my existence is wet, my ultimates dripping. But if I wanted to play the rebel, (and you can get quite a kick out of it, that I admit), I'd try it for size. And, if it didn't fit, I'd try another size. Cut your foot to fit your shoe, Bumbo. Take it easy; you're better off on your back.

Bumbo says,

There's no half-way here. I'd look pretty silly jumping ship at Gibraltar. I *feel* I should stick out before I start.

Jock says,

You feel a lot of things, one thing now, one thing later. But take it from me, boyo, the days of sacrificial lambs are past. The last lost sheep had their haemorrhages in Spain; only the poets weren't scratched. All this sins-of-the-world stuff gives me a pain in the arse. Take it as it comes, but don't stick your neck out for it.

Bumbo says,

Why the hell not? It's something at least I care about.

Jock says,

Do you? Or do you feel you *should* care about it? Aren't you past the old conscience-stricken-gentry stage? Rah for the British Raj. Hip, hip. Keep a straight bat; an Englishman's word is his Bearer Bond. Oh, be reasonable, man. Nobody in their senses wants the crooked made straight. It's the corkscrew that opens the bottle, ain't it? You bust the neck off, and you'll cut your mouth on the splinters. But don't listen to me, you horrible hero. I'm just a coffee-bar millionaire, whose home-spun wisdom wouldn't keep a flea in safety-pins for ten minutes.

Bumbo says,

You're pretty convincing.

Jock says,

Why? Because I talk so fast? Because my mouth's so big? Because my cracks are always wise? No. I'll tell you why. Because I say what you want to hear, the easy way out. Look, boyo, you can convince anyone, if you haven't got any convictions of your own. But if you have got convictions, what do you get but ten years' hard labour, plus the afterlife, with maybe a Jew's Harp at the end? Leave it to the morons, boy; don't you be bothered. Don't fuss. You can't do anything. If you really want to get on top of the whole cosmos, just let it get on top of you. That's the secret.

Don't expect what isn't. That's power. That's glory. That's the miracle of life. That's the essence of existence, the ultimate good, the absolute shower.

Bumbo says,

But I would be *somebody* then. At the moment, me, I'm nothing. Just a lot of faces with a draught behind. But I am determined. Nobody is going to push me around.

Jock says,

Does it matter if you're nothing? Enjoy the faces. Shift about. Like the act. Be an honest hypocrite. But don't fuss, don't make problems for you. All my eye to this human predicament lark. Do what the old globe makes it easiest for you to do, and think about liking it after. Keep six lines playing all at one time; they won't all snap at once. Hey, two cappucinos, Mac, and go easy on the froth.

Bumbo says,

You make it sound all so bloody easy.

Jock says,

That's right. But you're lovely and young yet, kiddo. You just stay Peter Pan, and I'll be your Tinkerbell, a little lamp burning in the night, guide, guardian and friend, to help you unstiffen that old upper lip, and keep your pecker down on the shit, where all the other poor bastards are.

10

BY THE WAY

When Bumbo, later, thought of the time before his breaking, that, in retrospect, seemed
so inevitable, he could only remember five
or six incidents taking place before the Hungarian
revolt; but the order of their happening he had
forgotten.

The first was that he checked Quartermaster-
Sergeant Issy's Stores for sports equipment, and found
articles missing to the value of £15 6s. 8½d. Sgt. (QM)
Issy swore it was no fault of his, but Bumbo, obeying
the Law, had him marched in before the Commanding
Officer, who ordered Sgt. (QM) Issy to repay the full
amount, with the loss of three months' seniority.

Secondly, the Regimental Lieutenant-Colonel's
inspection, the big parade of the year, when the working of the whole Battalion was rigorously examined,
was postponed from its normal time in July to
November, in view of the need to prepare the Battalion
for field-training, and immediate military action.

The third incident was a conversation that took
place one evening in the Mess, when his brother
Officers asked Bumbo what he did in his spare time.
My god, yes, Susie was a hell of a fruit, but why didn't

he take her to the Four Hundred, or the Berkeley, or somewhere reasonable? He couldn't spend all his time bouncing up and down with her. He had to eat.

I don't bounce up and down with Susie, in your sense of the word, Bumbo says, and I eat in Chelsea.

. . . You don't *do her*?

And you eat in *Chelsea*?

There's something queer about you, Bumbo.

It's all those King's Road palsy-walsies of yours. Why don't you put on a pair of silk knickers, and trip up and down, holding hands, in the fairy-ring on Chelsea Green?

Well, well, who'd have thought it? Hetero Bumbo is off with the harry homos. . . .

Bumbo says,

I think I should be in good company if I said, Homo Sum.

There is a long, long silence.

. . . Bloody clever.

Which of your gay friends thought that one up, and up where?

Bumbo says,

It's quite, quite original, like most of what I say and do.

Belleyes the Adjutant says,

Watch your step, Bumbo. Don't be too original. Officers in the Reds do not get involved in scandals.

Bumbo says,

Quite so. But I wear the uniform. I do my

duty. And if I want to paint my toenails green, what's it to you, so long as I wear my boots, and my servant has polished them satisfactorily?

Laughing Gus changed the conversation, saying, render to Welly B. the things which are Welly B.'s, which are gumboots, and etcetera. But Bumbo, finding the pose of the homosexual more and more expected of him, took a perverse pleasure in playing to the crowd. He would buy a bottle of Arpège for Susie, and keep it in his pocket, until he saw Farquhar. He would then put a little of the scent on the back of his hand, and hold it up to Farquhar's long nose, and say,

Isn't it absolute heaven? It's my very favourite.

Or else he would stick a carnation behind his ear, instead of in his buttonhole, and pitch his voice high, drawling,

Sensuous little blossoms, aren't they?

Bumbo knew he was being childish, but he miscalculated the effect of his actions. He did not know that the majors and the captains were planning revenge.

The fourth series of memories began in a lull during a kickabout in the park, with Sgt. Peters, and L/Sgts. Johnson and James, P. Bumbo went into a reverie, thinking of Susie, and only woke to the world, when Sgt. Peters tapped him on the shoulder, saying,

It's a beautiful face you've got on you, sir, as if Pearly Kings were whispering great thoughts in your ear, but shall we get on with the bleeding practice? There's a bloody great thundercloud spoiling the view.

But the two Lance-Sergeants had laughed kindly at him, as though they also had thought, sometimes, in the same way.

It was this dream of love (the product of his last loving night with Susie, and of his self-conviction by his letter to her), that made Bumbo blind to the truth. For the affair of Susie was running into the shallows.

Her reply was a short Letter-Postcard.

Darling,

You do write such *wonderful* letters. I *am* a lucky girl to get them. You *do* spoil me terribly. But I love to get them, so do write me another.

I'm afraid this is going to be my usual, brief scrawl, but you do know I simply can't express myself like you. Am off on another modelling job with lots of other lush thrushes, so am writing this on top of a bus, in a great hurry. See you Wednesday,

lots of love,

Susie X

Susie was working harder and harder. She saw Bumbo less and less. When she did see him, she was too tired to go to bed with him. Her kisses became almost mechanical, but their declaration of mutual love was a habit, as though they were married.

Bumbo did not wish to see that the situation had changed. He did ask Susie to marry him; he would give up Cambridge for her, and work in the City. Susie said she would think about it; but she now saw herself as Somebody, even when she was with Bumbo. But twice a week or so, they went out together to the movies

Susie liked; and the word "love" appeared frequently in their conversations.

Then, finally, the nightmare.

Bumbo had gone to bed early one evening, feeling exhausted. He fell asleep. He dreamed that his spirit was in Susie's body, which was dancing, naked, inside the apex of a vast horn of faces, one for each molecule, that ringed the dancing-girl round, ring below narrowing ring, from the black above. Bumbo-that-was-Susie finished the dance, and looked up the spiralled faces, to the green and gibbering Cerberus-mask, which babbled in the sky, Torment, take what you will, even unto half my kingdom, all my kingdom, which is tribulation.

Then the faces on the inside of the ring jeered and catcalled, as the side of the horn split. Four eunuchs' masks wobbled in, bearing a tray on their protruding tongues—Thistlethought, the Beater, the Sheik, and Buffo stuck out their tongues, as hands to hold up the tray, on which a face that was no face rested, a no-face that yet suggested a face, his own face, the no-face of Bumbo.

Bumbo screams, waking. Fright pins his heart to his ribs like a live bee. Someone is in the room.

Who's that, who's that, Bumbo jabbers. Who's that, or I'll kill you?

For God's sake, quiet down, says a voice.

Put on the light, or I'll kill you, I swear I will.

The light shines. Maypole Bean is standing by the door, looking foolish.

I just brought back that sword-belt of yours I borrowed. Sorry I disturbed you.

Bumbo lies back in his bed. He is shivering and sweating.

It's all right, he says. I must be feeling a bit nervous. I'm overtired. Good night, Bean.

Bean says, Good night, and goes out, switching off the light. Bumbo lies shaking in the darkness for a long time. He thinks of circling under the sheets, as he did, when he was a child. But it is too childish.

Eventually, he sleeps.

II

HEROICS BEGIN AT HOME

The week of the Hungarian revolution and the Suez ultimatum came. England's great, bleeding heart was exposed. She bled for the poor bleeding Hungarians, but she did nothing except send a little legal relief, and a few illicit undergraduates, to Budapest. She also bled for poor bleeding Israel; the persecuted Jews, the Chosen People, Balfour's black-eyed babies, must be saved, whatever the cost, from victory; in the name of peace and duty, Sir Anthony Eden sent the bombers into Suez.

And England's domestic haemorrhages also burst. The unpatriotic rage of the Universities, of Her Majesty's Opposition, and of even a section of the aristocracy, could not be wholly dismissed by the rulers, as red. Arabs beat up Bump Suppers in cloistered seats of learning; Members of Parliament shouted and yelled at each other like kiddies in a kindergarten; in the counties, old neighbours did no more than wish each other good morning—and even that topic of conversation was unsafe, depending on the news. But, most of all, England's people bled, from the inept propaganda of the Government, when the truth might have been more useful.

Bumbo's Battalion was put on a war footing, ready to move at twenty-four hours' notice. But Public Duties were still carried out. A ceremony is a ceremony, and must be done. Belleyes made a last check-up to ensure that the last half-inch of Bumbo's left trouser-leg was, at last, correctly adjusted before Guard Mounting.

Thus Bumbo, nervous, overtired, with diarrhoea in his emotions, irrationally seeking Death, Glory, Honour and The Hour of Decision in the far-flung battle-line, was sent on Queen's Guard, six hundred yards from Wellington Barracks, down the Mall, in a slight mist.

PART THREE

The Breaking of Bumbo

Men do not become what by nature they are meant to be, but what society makes them. The generous feelings, and high propensities of the soul are, as it were, shrunk up, seared, violently wrenched, and amputated, to fit us for our intercourse with the world, something in the manner that beggars maim and mutilate their children, to make them fit for their future situation in life.

WILLIAM HAZLITT

12

BUMBO IN BLUES

Bumbo sat on the broad, raised wooden fender in the Officer's Guard Room of St. James's Palace. Behind him, the portrait of the young Queen Victoria looked across the table, set with silver and glass and white napkins, and with the thirteenth authentic hoof of Napoleon's horse, Marengo, now made into a snuff-box. Bumbo sat, facing the historical screen, stuck over with coloured pictures, many years old, pictures of Pitt and musket-men and Redcoat heroics. Every so often, a drunk officer would take Marlborough's sword out of its glass case, and slash at the screen, and later pay for its repair.

There were five of them at dinner; Farquhar, and Farquhar's friend from the City; salacious Captain Jinks; and the Ensigns, Bumbo Bailey and Outram Utterluck. They had eaten borsch, oysters, pheasant, and rum soufflée. The port had been circulating for half-an-hour.

Farquhar's friend from the City was in oil, and he talked about oil. Shell and Suez. B.P. and Suez. Burmah and Suez. Men ruined, he said, because of Suez. City men, whose income had dropped hundreds a week, because of Suez. He didn't talk of the United Nations. Or Hungary. Or grouse-shooting. Or cars. Just about Suez; through soup, fish, meat, and pudding, about Suez.

. . . That bloody Nasser.

Just like Hitler.

We'll show him the lion's got a bite still.

All you've got to do with these tin-pot gyppos is show them a bit of the old jackboot. I know the wogs.

All we've done for them, too.

Ingratitude.

You know, we might see a bit of action soon, if we're lucky. I'm keeping my fingers crossed.

Bet old Nasser would move a bit, with a flamethrower on his tail. . . .

Bumbo speaks,

I like Nasser. I think he's a sound man.

They all look at him, as if his boots were squeaking during a sermon in Westminster Abbey.

. . . You don't mean that, Bumbo. You can't.

Dear old Bumbo. Difficult as usual.

You like Nasser? Why don't you go and take a jump into the Canal? . . .

Bumbo finishes his port, and pours out another glass. He speaks again.

I like Nasser. He's only behaving perfectly reasonably. He can't get his money, and he's got to get prestige to stay on top. So he puts the arm on us, and grabs the Canal. What can we do? Nothing, except take three months to put a few men in Cyprus. And wait. Then in goes Israel. In goes France. And in goes bumbling, stupid, hypocritical old England, pulling her punches. War with morals. I ask you. *War* with *morals*. Warning them to get off the airfields so they wouldn't be under the bombs we dropped. *Us? Moral?* And we've got into every war in the last two hundred years we could have, in the name of peace. All through the nineteenth century we've got the biggest standing army in the world in India, and what do we do? Palmerston and Liberalism, Gladstone and Freedom, bellyaching about the peaceable English till they make us believe their crap. Peaceable? Us? If you gave an Englishman a baby's rattle, he'd try to choke you by ramming it back down your throat.

Farquhar speaks,

Bailey, you're drunk.

But Bumbo is now speaking woe to his Israel; like a prophet from the hills, he shouts, Ichabod, thy glory is departed.

. . . Yes, I'm drunk. I'm tight. I'm stinking. I'm a bum. But these days you've got the bums in with you. Bumbo the Bum. And this bum isn't going to fight in any bummy, phoney war. . . .

Bumbo stands up. Bumbo bangs his fist on the table.

. . . I didn't ask to come in this. Two years I've got to do. You can get my body, by Christ, but you're not going to get me. I'm not going to fight in any phoney bleeding war for any phoney bleeding England. We're going to get slapped now. We've been slapping everyone since Napoleon, and now it's our turn to be slapped, and, by God, I hope they slap us hard. . . .

No one interrupts. They gawp at Bumbo, mouths open but silent.

. . . And when they slap back, what does moral old Britain do? Turn the other cheek? Like hell. Back we go, back to the garden of Eden. Discipline, men, close the ranks. Form hollow squares. Down with the fuzzy-wuzzies. Don't fire till you see the whites of their eyes. The Gatling's jammed, but, dammit, give them the cold steel. They're wogs, nigs, the sons of Ham, under God, Albion, and ruddy Kipling. . . .

They still stare, manners tying their tongues and incomprehension their movements.

. . . O.K. Suppose we beat Egypt. We lose anyway. We've got to sell ourselves to live, and who'll buy Johnny Bull, with a Boer War musket in his hand? We don't want our Empire, say we (minus Beaverbrook). Give it away, as long as you still buy British. We only want to trade. We don't want to fight. Cyprus —a police action. Kenya—restoring order. Got to protect British lives. Oh, we think we're so damn wonderful still. And all we are is a lousy punch-drunk ex-champ, between a couple of real big men, jockeying around for the K.O., not caring two damn hoots about us. One swift back-hander from either of them, and we're on the canvas. But, by Christ, we can make such a big bang when we fall. We can make the biggest bloody bang they've ever seen. And then the big men will make big bangs too, and we'll all sit around pulling crackers, bang, bang, bang, bang, till we're all dead, but great, wonderful, heroic, unbeaten Britain, didn't she go out with a bang!

Farquhar gets up. At last, anger. Splendid, red-faced, righteous, fair-moustached British anger. The real home-made article, contained, wrapped up in packets for company.

Bailey, you're drunk. Go to bed. I'm ordering you to go to bed. There's a guest here, remember. Think of the Regiment. Outram, take that bloody fool Bumbo away before I lose my temper.

Bumbo allows Outram to take him out of the room, and lead him up the stairs to the Ensign's bedroom. He sits on the bed. Outram stands beside him.

Outram speaks,

Are you all right now?

Bumbo speaks,

Yes, I'm all right. It's the first time I've been all right for a long time. But the trouble is, that you're all right too. You're all, always, all so bloody right. With you, it's me that's wrong. And I half agree with you, I'm wrong. In this set-up, which couldn't be righter, I'm wrong.

Outram speaks,

Oh, I don't know. You're just a bit drunk. There's nothing much right or wrong in that. You'll feel better in the morning.

Bumbo speaks,

That's it. I *will* feel better in the morning. I'll say I'm sorry, and bloody Farquhar will be oh-so-bloody nice, and say, that's all right, Bumbo, I understand. You don't know what you're saying when you're pickled. You don't mean a word you say when you're oiled. But I *do*. It's what I *do* mean. Do I have to get pickled now every time I want to say something?

Outram speaks,

Of course not, Bumbo. That's the nice thing about you. You may talk a hell of a lot of bloody nonsense, but at least I can always tell you really think what you say.

Bumbo speaks,

You think so? You think, honest old Bumbo, he'll tell you the truth? Just because I look like Christ crucified, or something? It's all a damn lie. I talk rich with you; and when I talk poor, it's only because I *am* poor, and I can't stand your being so lousy rich, so I want to get at you, and I talk poor. Because it makes you feel uncomfortable. Do you think, honest old Bumbo? Have you ever met a man who was really poor, and proud of it? If so, show me where they put him up against a wall, and shot him.

Outram speaks,

Don't be so self-dramatic. Everybody lies. You've no need to worry yourself. You're more honest than most.

Bumbo speaks,

But that's what I *won't* be. Who the hell wants to be more honest than *most*? What's *most* got to do with me? The moment a man says, I'm one of a crowd, he might as well be dead.

Outram speaks,

O.K. You can stick out, if you like. But you can't blame us for making things difficult for you. I mean, there's no reason why you shouldn't be different *inside* the world you're born into.

Bumbo speaks,

I grant you that. But I wasn't born into your world. I arrived there by sheer chance. At the age of ten, I met a little boy in a park, and I said to him, what's the best school there is, and he says, Eton, stupid, and so I say, I'll go there. And I do.

Outram speaks,

Give it time, Bumbo. You've only got to last out another ten months, and then you *can* get out, and let us all go to hell our own sweet way.

Bumbo says,

But it's too late. The one thing I haven't got is time. Every day, can't you see, it's more and more certain I can't get away. You've got a man-trap on one leg of me; I can only walk on the other. And in another four months I'll be crawling. I may be crawling already. And this Suez business. What am I going to do, if they send us off?

Outram says,

Maybe they won't. Anyway, what good does it do, one man sticking out against it?

Bumbo says,

I don't know. I just don't know. But every so often, one man's just got to stick out.

Outram says,

Why should it be you?

Bumbo says,

I wish it didn't have to be. But who else?

Outram says,

Nobody else. But I respect you for it.

Bumbo says,

Sure you respect me. But when did other people's respect get them court-martialled with you? When did other people's admiration make them sign a blank cheque for your future conduct?

Outram says,

    I can't help you, Bumbo. I just can't help you.

Bumbo says,

    No one can, but me. But you're a nice guy, Outram. You're a really nice guy.

Outram says,

    Phooey.

Bumbo says,

    But you are, you see. You're rich enough to be nice. You're secure enough to be pleasant. Being kind just comes natural to you. Outram Utterluck, the Great Commoner; Dinkley Manor, yacht at Cowes, Jag., account at Coutts. Take it all away, Outram, and would you be so nice? It's not a question, you know, of affording to be nice. Everyone's as nice as they can afford to be; it's just the rich who can afford rather more.

Outram says,

    Good night, Bumbo. I'll tell the sergeant to send up the drummer-boy to call you before your rounds. I must be getting back to the Palace.

Bumbo says,

    If you were poor, Outram, if you got rid of all your stuff and didn't have anything to lose, wouldn't you stick it out with me?

Outram says,

    Good night, Bumbo.

Outram goes out of the door. Bumbo lies on his bed, and closes his eyes. Outside, he can hear the sentry, crash, crash, crash, trying to turn softly outside the Officer's Guardroom, so as not to disturb them.

Good night, Outram.

Bumbo speaks, but Outram is already gone. There is only the noise of the sentry's heels on the tar, heel after heel, boot after boot, boots, boots, boots, boots, marching up and down again. And always just the right boot. Right, right, right. Pick up the step there. No left boot. No wrong boot. Only the right boot. Right. Right. Always bloody right.

13

UNLUCKY FOR SOME

The Guard dismounted on Thursday. Bumbo had a fit of the trembles, standing to attention in the forecourt of Buckingham Palace. His leg began to shake uncontrollably, and the shaking ran up his thighs to the muscles of his back, and to the arm that held up the Colour in its belt, so that the pole shook and swayed, as though there was a high wind blowing on that still day. Farquhar had to hurry his commands, terrified that Bumbo was about to faint.

Once the dismount was over, and they had returned to the Officers' Mess, Farquhar was surprisingly kind to Bumbo, telling him not to be a ruddy fool, to wake his ideas up, to take a pull on himself, and to buck up generally. He was not going to report Bumbo to the Adjutant, for moving on parade; but if Bumbo put a foot wrong on the Regimental Lieutenant-Colonel's Inspection on Monday, he, Farquhar, would know the reason why.

Bumbo began to drink at lunch. He had accepted for a Bar Society dance at the Inner Temple that night; Sheila had suddenly telephoned at the last moment, and said, Would he come? Some one must have fallen down on her. But Bumbo accepted. He hadn't got enough money to do anything else that night, and Susie was in Brighton, advertising razor-blades. Thank God he was taking the Rugby League team to the north on Friday: he could probably manage a fiver for that. Sgt. Peters had arranged a League game at last, against the only other Army League team in England— the Pay Corps. As playing the League was forbidden in the Army anyway, and only Rugby Union allowed (thirteen-a-side in the League, instead of fifteen-a-side; professional, as opposed to the so-called *amateur* Union), the Reds were playing the Pay Corps for the unofficial championship of the Army. They were to play a curtain-raiser, beginning at one o'clock, before the big Cup game, Leeds v. Halifax, at two-thirty on the Saturday; a crowd of twenty thousand was expected; a silver collection would be taken on the ground to pay for the expense of the bus there and back. For, in Bumbo's view, irrespective of the enormous recruiting appeal—the Reds recruited chiefly in Yorkshire—the labourer was openly worthy of his hire.

Bumbo, finding nothing to do that afternoon in the Company, went on drinking; he wouldn't have to pay his Mess bill for three weeks. He wrote twenty bread-and-butter letters that had been piling up during the last month, and then went upstairs to have a bath, and to change into tails for the evening. He arrived punctually at Sheila's parents': eight-fifteen for eight-thirty.

Sheila was as white as a fish-belly all dinner. Her brightness was pathetic to watch, her cosmetic-mask badly put on. From time to time, Bumbo saw her looking straight and vacant ahead of her, as though, for once, she was in another world than the immediate one around her.

Bumbo kept on drinking steadily, gin, champagne, brandy. But he was getting drunk-depressed, drunk-silent. For the conversation throughout dinner remained carefully clear of the danger-topic. Society had decided to forget Suez; God knows, it was enough trouble as it was, trying to keep up pretences on dwindling incomes, trying to scratch up the illusion of grandeur on sixpence, without finding the last unbuyable, unbreachable, inimitable bastion of the good old English way of life, the dinner party conversation, at the mercy of controversy. Argument at the table was like a cock among hens, possible, even natural, but always unmentionable. The last thing left to a gentleman was to talk like one. And it wasn't only a matter of the B.B.C. accent, whatever the ruddy Socialists said. Conversation was an art, dying maybe; but, like ju-jitsu, it was more than an exercise; it implied a philosophy, and a whole way of life. It was the nuances under the seeming-nothing of the hackneyed phrases that the Old Guard could not teach to the Angry Young Men. Everything now was so bloody explicit. But, in the candlelight, even the subject of God was preferable to Suez, or silence.

When, at last, the dinner party arrived at the Hall of the Inner Temple, Sheila grabbed hold of Bumbo. *Don't* leave me, for *God's* sake, she said. I just *couldn't stand* it. I've *got* to talk to you. *Please.*

Bumbo had never seen Sheila look so ugly. He thought it wasn't *Pretty please* now. Just *Plain please.* Very *Plain please.*

They queued up to be introduced, shook the limp hands of whoever it was who stood there to have their hands shaken, and jolted their way once round the floor. They pushed their way back through the door. Sheila had left her coat on a table. They went out, past the old retainer, set to guard the main entrance.

Bumbo, thinking it might be a good plan, and cheaper, to come back, decided to talk to the old retainer. He said,

You remember me, don't you? '49.

The old retainer peered up at Bumbo.

Oh, yes, sir. Distinctly, sir. I couldn't ever forget you, sir.

Bumbo had never seen him before.

Bumbo and Sheila did not speak at all, until they reached the Embankment, where they leaned on a wall overlooking the Thames. Bumbo used to pass the spot each time he marched with the Picquet to the Bank.

Well, said Bumbo.

Sheila looked at him, the area of her eyes waxing and waning, her face working, like instant moons in a scudding sky.

Sheila says,

I don't know *how* to tell you. I haven't *really* seen you since *that* time. Don't you remember?

Bumbo says, hardly recollecting,

I remember perfectly.

Sheila says,

Do you? You *really did* like me then, didn't you? You *really did*.

Bumbo says,

Yes, I did. *Really*, I did.

Sheila says,

Then you aren't going to *mind* what I'm going to tell you, *are* you? *Promise* me you won't mind. If you don't *promise* me, I'm not going to *tell* you.

Bumbo thought it was too ridiculous. He was being made to apologize for being a father-confessor. He wondered whether it was the function of a failed seducer to become guide, guardian and friend. Presumably yes; even attempted crime had its punishment.

Bumbo says,

I promise I won't tell. Cross my heart. On the Book. Everything.

Sheila says,

You *really, truly mean* you *won't* tell.

Bumbo says,

I really, truly mean I won't tell.

Sheila says,

Oh, I *can't* tell you. You'll *hate* me for telling you. I know you're simply going to *loathe* me for telling you.

Bumbo is bored. He says,

Look, it doesn't make any difference *what* you tell me. But if you're going to say something, just say it. Or back we go to the dance.

Bumbo looks out over the river. A late double-decker bus, carrying home pressmen from Fleet Street, rides the curve of the parapet of Blackfriars Bridge. The lamp-lights throw wavy-yellow commas in reflection on the water. Bumbo puts an arm round Sheila, trying to get his story; but she only cries. Even in the confessional, she still manages to keep off the point. Eventually she says,

I'm *going* to have a *baby*.

A joke jumps irrelevantly into Bumbo's mind. A deb. is talking to her escort, as they lean over the side of a bridge. Darling, she says, if I have a baby, I'm going to throw myself in the river. And he replies, he replies what Bumbo finds himself replying, aloud,

How very good of you, darling.

Sheila sounds angry. Her voice is suddenly sharp.

I *said* I was going to have a *baby*.

Bumbo says,

Oh yes. So you were. Well, I suppose you'd better get married or something.

Sheila says,

But I don't *want* to *marry* him. I wouldn't *dream* of *marrying him*. He's an *undergraduate*. At *Oxford*. I simply *couldn't* marry him. Now, you *promised*. You aren't going to *tell* any one, are you? I'll *kill* myself if you do. I *will*.

Bumbo manages to choke back the deb. joke this time, and says,

Well, you can't really keep it dark all that long, you know. It sort of grows upon you. What would the parents say?

Sheila says,

They'll *kill* me. I know they'll simply *murder* me.

Bumbo says,

There seems to be an awful lot of killing going on. I don't think it can be really as bad as that, you know. It's all very natural, you see. Why don't you just have the little brute, and lump it? They can't really do anything to you.

Sheila says,

But what *would* my *friends* say? And *mummy's* friends? Oh. . . .

Sheila began to cry again. Bumbo let her cry, and looked idly at the water. He thought he saw a corpse in the river, but it was only a half-sunk cereals carton, slowly drifting downstream on the tide. He wished Sheila would hurry up, and get over with it. He rubbed his hand vaguely on her shoulders.

Sheila says,

I thought there was a way of getting *rid* of babies. *He* said it's as easy as an *appendix*. Much *safer* too. Not to worry. But then he went *away*.

Bumbo was tired to death. The drink sat on his head like his bearskin. He felt a dull anger.

Bumbo says,

So he just walked out and left you. Charming bastard. And he shot you that line about appendix? Look, Sheila, you *have* that baby. It won't kill you. You've had your fun. You carry the can for it. That's the trouble with all you lot, you won't carry the can. Have the thing. Just have it.

Sheila cries,

I thought you were *nice*. I thought you'd *help*. I thought you'd *know* about these things. You're being *horrid*. *Beastly*.

Bumbo says, weary to death, what is expected of him.

Stop crying, honey. Go on, stop crying.

I'll arrange it all for you, if you want it that way. I'll fix it up. I'll borrow the money for you. It's quite simple, and it never hurts any one. My friends have to fix it up every second day. It'll be all right. I know it will.

Sheila puts both of her arms around Bumbo, and hugs him. She says,

You're *sweet*, Bumbo. I *knew* you'd do it. Oh, you're so *sweet*, Bumbo. I *do* love you, Bumbo, I *really do*. But you *won't* tell *any* one, will you? All you men together, you're worse than us girls. You *won't*, *will* you? *Promise* me you *won't*?

Bumbo says,

I promise. I'll ring you up on Tuesday morning, early, when I've fixed it. I can't do it before. I've got to go away. Is that all right?

Sheila says,

Heaven, Bumbo. Simply heaven. Oh, Bumbo, I *do* love you.

Sheila chatters the whole way back to the dance. Bumbo doesn't have to talk at all. He just has to nod his head every so often. Death and birth seem equally easy to fix and to forget. Perhaps even Bumbo himself could have a shot at his own renaissance.

They got back to the dance. The old retainer respectfully remembered them. Sheila went to the Ladies Room; Bumbo was called to the bar. He began drinking his way through a tray of full champagne-glasses. He drank each glass, holding it in his left hand, and, with the forefinger of his right hand, he stirred the bubbles out of the other glasses. Looking down over the edge of the white cloth on the bar-table, he saw a small, long-haired, dirty, scruffy Pekinese lifting his leg in disdain among the empty bottles.

God knows how you got in here without a ticket, Bumbo said out loud, but I couldn't agree with you more.

Looking round again, Bumbo saw Sheila remorselessly cutting her way through the crowd towards him, like an ice-breaker through the pack-ice in the Far North. He couldn't stand it. He sat down on the floor, and crawled under the bar-table. The Pekinese was already there before him. It licked his nose.

My friend, said Bumbo, my dear friend. I bet you're the wisest hound that never got to Crufts.

He licked the dog's nose back.

The cloth, that covered the far side of the table, was lifted up. Bumbo could dimly see the face of the barman, upside down.

Bumbo says,

Hi.

The barman says,

The young lady asked me to ask you if you was all right down there, sir.

Bumbo says,

Fine, I'm just doing fine down here.

The cloth is dropped back. Bumbo and the Peke continue to lick each other happily. The cloth is lifted again.

The barman says,

The young lady says it will ruin her dress if she comes down and joins you, sir, but what are you doing down there?

Bumbo says,

I'm composing a speech for the Vets Dinner, and an old acquaintance of mine here has kindly consented to help me with my labours.

The cloth is dropped back. Bumbo is beginning to feel a little cramped. And so, tucking the Peke under one arm, he crawls out the far side of the bar, bumping into the face of the barman, who is coming down for the third time.

The barman says,

Ah, there you are, sir. I thought we'd lost you for ever. The young lady says, why don't you make your speech up here?

Bumbo stands up. Bumbo says,

So I will, Mac, so I will.

Bumbo climbs onto the table. He stands up, still holding the Peke in his arms. And Bumbo says,

Ladies and gentlemen. . . .

Behind him, the barman says,

You can't do that here, sir.

Bumbo says,

Of course, I can. I can do anything, anywhere. I'm Bumbo. And Bumbo can do anything, anywhere. Can't he?

He throws out his hands wide to the audience of drinkers, who are now all looking at him. They shout, Bumbo. Bumbo. Speech. Speech. The Peke drops on to the table, barking.

Bumbo declaims,

Ladies and gentlemen, me and my friend here . . . (*laughter*) . . . me and my friend have come to talk to you on a matter of the gravest importance. . . .

(*cheers*). . . . My friend expressed himself recently dissatisfied with the present state of affairs . . . (*loud cheers*) . . . shortly, pungently, he stated that the whole joint stank . . . (*louder cheering*) . . . stank to high heaven. And it's not good enough. It's not good enough at all. Ladies and gentlemen, it wasn't only the joint that stank. You stank too. In fact, said my friend, you stank worse. (*Silence*) Ladies and gentlemen, me and my friend thought, if that was the case, it would be a good thing if you threw yourselves out, and threw the whole joint out with you . . . don't you. . . .

At this moment, Bumbo felt himself falling. With the sound of Armageddon, the table underneath him broke, sliding a couple of hundred champagne-glasses, sixteen plates of sandwiches, three jugs of orange juice, eight bowls of strawberries, and many other etceteras, to a point that was Bumbo Recumbent. And it was the sign for a most regrettable scene. The cultivated young men, the finished young women, budding barristers, shining solicitors, all began throwing at each other anything that came to hand. The Inner Temple, the home of the Law, was a plethora of flying paraphernalia, handbags, sausages, gloves, carnations, lighted cigarettes, shoes. The budding barristers and their dowager ladies, after a vain attempt to quell the riot, fled from the Hall, and the old retainer, the last representative of the old Law, was wrapped up in a table-cloth, blessed with a bottle of champagne poured over his head, and bundled down the steps.

In peace, covered with broken glass and strawberries, Bumbo slept the sleep of the just.

14

SOLD DUMMY

They kicked off in the empty Leeds stadium at five minutes past one on Saturday. Perhaps thirty soldiers, from the Pay Corps, stood in a knot on one of the terraces, a minute filling on the bare tooth of the huge mouth of the ground, which gaped open to the lead of the sky above. The Reds' only supporter was Sgt. Issy, who had come with the team to look after the baggage, and act as touch-judge.

After a couple of minutes, a short punt-ahead came to Bumbo at full-back. He picked up the ball cleanly, dropped it down onto his swinging instep, and made a competent short touch, second-bounce. One of the Pay Corps, following up fast, caught Bumbo in the face with a flat palm, a full second after Bumbo had got rid of the ball. Bumbo bounced backwards onto the ground, and got up again, feeling angry as hell, wiping the blood off his lip with the back of his hand.

Bumbo says,

Can't you tackle low, you crummy bastard?

The Pay Corps man laughs, and runs on. Christ, what bastards. Bumbo clenches his fists, and concentrates on pumping out anger from the wound on his lip, pumping out, into the stream of his blood, synthetic hate.

Bumbo shouts,

Bounce these bastards.

Sgt. Issy laughs from the touch line. But the Pay Corps keep coming through. The Reds line across the field badly; they miss their tackles; when they are brought down, they throw the ball away, instead of dying with it, and keeping possession of it for a quick heel from the two-man scrum that follows a tackle. The Pay Corps keep coming through, so that Bumbo is always tackling, falling, dying, rising, swearing, shouting, kicking and crouching, always waiting for the break-through that only comes one time in ten, and then, when it comes, it's always two or three of *Them*. Feint at the first. Hope he drops the ball, so you can fall on it. He doesn't. It's a quick pass to number two. A bad pass. He takes it, standing still. Jump him, round the shoulders, so he can't throw it away. But he does. Number three drops it, boots it on ahead. But it's a knock-on, a scrum-down. Get up. Back to position. There's L/Cpl. Simons at fly-half, who says,

Oh, bloody good, sir, bloody good.

And, by Christ, he means it. It's not just Ensign Bailey, 2/Lt. Bailey, Bailey to be buttered up, because he's a lousy officer. It's Man Bumbo, full-back, the last ditch in the way of the bloody Pay Corps, who are going to get bloody well thumped, as long as Bumbo, bleeding, can stand.

Bumbo wipes his hand across his lip again. Blood still. That's good. He drags his hand across his shirt, wishing that the blood would show clearly on the cloth to imply that Bumbo was still carrying on, although suffering from severe internal injuries. Unfortunately, the Reds played in scarlet, which was good for recruiting, if not heroics.

Bumbo throws back his head, hoping the ground is fuller. Yes, there must be a couple of hundred there now.

But the Pay Corps keep on coming through. They score three times, one goal, two tries. The Reds are 11–0 to the bad. But the crowd is only shouting for the Reds.

Half-time. Sgt. Issy comes over with a wooden tray, covered with segments of cut lemon. Bumbo bites down into his slice. It tastes like vinegar. His mouth goes dry, his lips pucker on the inside, saliva runs into his mouth to dilute the acid. He swallows two, three times. He puts the rind of the lemon back on the tray.

L/Cpl. Thompson says,

We'll do those bleeders yet.

Sgt. Peters says,

By Christ, we will. Only eleven down. Two goals, and a try. We'll get that, easy. You've been playing a good game, sir.

Bumbo says, feigning modesty,

Not good enough, Sarnt Peters. But we're going to do better next half. We're going to take the pants off them. But get your men *low*. That's all we've got to do. Tackle them low.

The referee comes over. He blows his whistle. The teams change ends, line up again for the kick-off.

The ground is filling up fast. There must be at least a couple of thousand now.

From the kick-off, Gdsn. Bart catches the ball, and begins his run. Three of the Pay Corps get him, bring him down. One of them stands upright, and kicks Bart as he lies on the ground. Bart gets up, holding his knee. The crowd boo. The referee blows his whistle, gives a penalty.

Sgt. Peters says,

Oh, the bleeding bastards. The bleeding, bleeding bastards.

After that, it's a long maul. The Reds hit, kick, hold in the scrums. They crash the Pay Corps with their shoulders, put a boot in their backs when they are brought down. And the swelling, roaring, partisan crowd howls at the fight. It's the Reds, Reds, Reds. The first of the Pay Corps goes off, hopping on one leg, his arm round a helper. The crowd cheers. He doesn't come back. The second goes, crushed between Red and Red. Broken leg. The crowd is silent. Gdsn. Matt bullocks over near the posts. 11–3. Bumbo converts. 11–5. The Pay Corps come back with the kick-off, surging, breaking to the 25. And their wing gets the ball, stepping high, brushing off the hands of the stoppers, as Bumbo runs across to squeeze him in to the touch line. And he steps past Bumbo, who half-twists, falls, and, with the tips of his clutching fingers, flicks at his heel, so that he stumbles, trips over with the force of his running, and smashes down into touch two yards from the line, and five from the fallen Bumbo. Bumbo picks himself up, and as the crowd crescendoes in his ears, he smiles at the thunder of his blood. But, oh god, for some more breath.

At the scrum, the Reds heel, and the scrum-half is away. The ball sweeps straight along the line; and, through the gap that the Pay Corps leave—for now they are only eleven—the Reds' centre thunders, mad-scarlet, low-running as a bird-dog. He grounds the ball under the bar. Voices batter wild and loud, and hush, as Bumbo walks back from Bart, balancing the ball between his hands, as Bumbo wipes the toe of his boot on his leg, as Bumbo turns, as Bumbo takes five slow paces, as Bumbo swings his leg to send the ball turning, arse over tip, in a lazy parabola between the posts. 11–10. Voices crash out again, and keep up a muffled rumble; reverberate, the mouth of the ground breathes into the echoing lead lid of the sky.

The Reds thrust on. And, from a tight scrum, there is a sudden scream. They break. A Pay Corps forward is holding his elbow with his other hand. His shoulders are suddenly grotesque; the left has dropped six inches below the right. He walks off, his collarbone snapped. The crowd murmurs. Thirteen against ten. Five more minutes. No mercy, Reds, no mercy.

From the penalty, the Pay Corps make touch first-bounce, and, straining like madmen, heel. They pick up the ball and die; they heel, pick up the ball, and die; again, and again, and again; they will not lose the ball. The minutes pass. Bumbo runs forward. He stands be-hind the two-man scrum. The Pay Corps man drops the ball on to his foot, heels yet again. But his scrum-half fumbles. Bumbo gets his boot to the ball, kicks it ahead. Follow. Follow. Follow me, Reds. He stoops, as the ball bounces lucky and high, and gathers it into his chest. *They* hold him. He stumbles. But he stands. He moves. *They* let him go. He runs. Behind him, pass, pass. No, hang on. One of *Them* is there, ahead. Swerve right. As the face falls in, smack out with the left hand. Squash his nose with the heel of the thumb, until there is nothing against the hand. And the force of the hand-off hurls the corner-flag towards you. Fall, fall towards the white line. Fall on the ball, that is over the white line. And, as you fall, *They* hit you from the left, sending you skidding circular across the mud, to strike the pole of the flag. Splinter, pole. Break, wood. Drive, deep drive pain stab lance into his side. Roar, people of the crowd; thunder, sound in his ears. Weep, Bumbo, sitting sick, hand to his ribs, hand to the tear in his shirt, that grows darker with the spread of the slow stain.

They give Bumbo a handkerchief to hold against his side, and two of *Them* cross hands to make him a chair. *They* carry him to the dressing-room, and sit him on a bench. There he sits, gulping, until *They* bring a doctor to him, a cheerful, round, bluff doctor, who cuts back his shirt, swabs his wound, puts on lint and iodine and thick strips of plaster, and says,

There you are. Nothing to worry about. Just take it easy for a couple of days.

Bumbo dresses slowly, hunched against the throb of pain in his side. One by one, the men come up to him, to congratulate him. But now he is the officer again, not the man; and they are circumspect, almost shy, more happy swearing to each other. Bumbo goes up the stairs, and an attendant takes him to the director's box. *They* put a tumbler of neat whisky in his hand, and say, Well played, well played, wonderful game, it'll do you a lot of good round these parts, until Bumbo, feeling sick, has to go. He walks around outside the ground, and sits in the bus, waiting for the rest of the team to join him. When they come, they drive back to the neighbouring barracks. Bumbo leaves them, and goes to his bed in the Officers' Mess. He orders a bottle of brandy, but leaves it unopened. He lies there until next morning, hardly sleeping.

At opening-time on the Sunday evening, the bus reached the outskirts of London. The whole way down the Great North Road, the team had been singing, joking, smoking and drinking. Only two of the bus-load didn't join in the party. Bumbo sat silent, softly touching the plaster on his ribs, thinking over and over again about Suez, and taking slugs out of the bottle of brandy he had bought in Leeds. And the bus-driver was in a foul temper; it was a new bloody bus, first time out, as he kept on saying, and he wasn't going to have cigarette-burns all over the seats, and sweet-papers all over the floor.

Bumbo took out his wallet, and looked at the five pounds inside. They had won, after all. He really should do something about it. But he felt so dozy, so dizzy, so done, and the brandy fumed in his stomach like a smog.

Bumbo says to the driver,

Hey, driver, stop at the next pub we come to. We're all going to have a drink.

The driver goes on for about three miles. There

is a pub, called "The Dog and Duck", which gives him a rake-off on drinks sold to coach-parties. He stops the bus in the car park outside.

The driver says,

Here you are, sir. And I can get us a room all on our own. I've been here before, and I know the ropes. It's the best pub on the whole road. You trust me.

They go inside, and up a flight of stairs, brushing past dried fronds of fern in Victorian pots, edging beneath the stuffed heads of caribous and moose, until they come to a brown-painted door, on which is hung a cardboard notice, COMMERCIAL ROOM. They enter. As the bus-driver had said, they have the place to themselves. The bus-driver goes away, to collect his commission from the landlord.

Bumbo says,

Well, beer all round?

All say, yes. L/Cpl. Thompson presses the knob of a bell, set in the chocolate wallpaper by the grate. An old man appears, and takes their order. Bumbo has another drink out of his bottle, and passes it round. He doesn't know whether he's drunk or dead. Perhaps both. But this disembodied hour seems as good a time as any for Bumbo's Moment of Truth, if any truth lasts longer than the moment.

Bumbo says,

Sarnt Peters, and what do you think about this Suez business? Suppose the battalion gets its marching orders, what do you think about that? I mean, what do you think about that?

Sgt. Peters says,

I don't know, sir. I was out with the
Battalion in the Canal Zone eighteen months ago, and
I didn't like it one bit. Those wogs, they're a nasty
thieving lot. If you give them a fag, they'll whip the
whole packet, and probably take your bleeding hand
with it.

Bumbo says,

So you wouldn't mind, if we had to go
tomorrow?

Sgt. Peters says,

I'd mind all right, sir. It's so bleeding hot
and sticky, and not a skirt in miles.

Bumbo, finding Sgt. Peters playing his lead, opens
it up.

And the rest of you, how do *you* feel about
going?

All speak, following each other, after the first
pause for thought.

. . . Not too bad, sir.

I don't think the wife would like it
much, sir.

I wouldn't mind having a bash at 'em.

You don't know your bleeding luck,
cocky, being here. You wait till you get out to that
godforsaken howling desert, and you'll want to get
straight on the first ship home to bleeding Blighty.

Anyway, they won't fight. It'll all be over
by the time we get there.

You're a hopeful bleeding bleeder,
aren't you, mate. . . .

Bumbo looks at the lost sheep, Mary's little lambs
following their master, and says,

In other words, you're not really too keen on going?

Sgt. Issy says, quiet and careful,

Well, there's not much option, is there, sir?

Bumbo says,

And what do you think about Suez? Do you think it's a good thing, or a bad thing?

The old man comes in at the door, with a tray of pint beer-mugs in his hand, and some packets of potato crisps. They take their drinks, crunch their crisps, and say,

Here's health.

Sgt. Issy says,

What do you mean, a good thing or a bad thing, sir?

This is the 64,000-dollar question. Quiz Kid Bumbo rubs his chin, knowing that the answer marks the point of no return, if there's any point at all. There must be some point; conviction begins at home, or else there's no sale abroad. He says, tiredly,

What I want to know is this. Do you think it's *right* for us to go and get killed, just to get back a bit of sand that belongs to the Egyptians anyway? Do you think it's *right* for us to pile in with the French and Israelis, and wipe out Nasser and the boys, just because they've made us look a bit silly? If you do, O.K., let 'em have it. It's not the first time guys have got it in the guts for nothing.

There is a silence. Then Gdsn. Andrewes says,

It's not for us, sir, to think about that. It's for you, sir, to give the orders. You've got education, sir. We just do as we're bloody well told.

Bumbo yawns to hear the soldier's answer, to do as he is told. No responsibility for anyone, only for Drunk Bumbo. Personal commitment is sold in brandy-bottles, for private consumption only.

Bumbo says, blurred,

Yes, I've got bloody education. But you can't shift it all on to me, Andrewes. You're a *man* too. You've got *choice* too. All of you have. Do *you* think it's right to go, Sarnt Peters?

Sgt. Peters says,

I don't ask any questions. I just do as Standing Orders say.

Bumbo tries the word, the word of power little children are stopped from saying under the pretence that it is rude.

Why?

Sgt. Peters says,

Because I'm told. It's more than my bleeding life's worth, if I don't.

Bumbo says,

And what is your bleeding life worth? A bullet in your head at Suez?

There is another silence. Sgt. Issy says,

You wouldn't be suggesting, sir, that we might refuse to go?

Gdsn. Thad the Lad says,

Not a mutiny, sir. Not like those Reservist Thistles over at Pirbright. Nor that lot in Malta.

Bumbo says,

Look, I can trust you all, can't I? You've trained with me. You played with me yesterday up at Leeds. You know I'm not going to let you down. You

K   145

do know that, don't you? I'm speaking as one of you, mind you, not as a bloody officer.

All say, Yessir. Yessir. They speak as if they were answering a command.

Bumbo rubs his hands across his eyes, trying to remember the schoolboy-hero phrases that he uses, when he is trying to convince soldiers.

You don't know how important you are. Nobody can fight if the army won't. You really don't know how important you are. It's just got to take you thirteen and me to march in for Battalion Orders, and say, we're not going to any bleeding Canal, and what happens? We go to the guardroom. Yes, but what else happens? A report goes to the War Office, saying the Reds, led by their *officers*, are out on mutiny. And also a letter goes to the papers from me, saying *why*. Half the country's on our side as it is. And when the Reds *and* their officers go out on mutiny, boy, is Old England coming to an end? We've won every bloody battle for the Establishment in three hundred years. It's time we asked *why*. And I can tell you, you may *think* you're nothing, but thirteen men, who won't do what they think is wrong, who will do what they think is right, and suffer for it, can change the face of the whole bleeding world.

Bumbo hears himself talking, but the voice doesn't seem to be his. It is as though he were rehearsing his own arguments aloud to the thirteen men, and not even convincing himself. But the voice has been slurring on, beyond his power to stop.

L/Sgt. James P. says,

What about the wife and the kids? They

146

wouldn't manage too good, if I were put away for five years.

Bumbo keeps on talking,

They can't starve in this country. That's the one thing it *does* do for you. And there's a time, Sarnt James, when every man's got to put what he believes in before every other bloody thing, person, whatever you like. It comes to most people once or twice, this moment, when they should stick out. And what happens? They look the other way. They run out on themselves. And you, none of you are cowards. Is any of you going to say to me, I'm yellow, I can't take it?

Blah, blah, blah. Bumbo wonders to hear his mouth string platitudes, when he doesn't even think he's thinking.

Gdsn. Thompson says,

It does look, sir, as if we was yellow, if we said we wasn't going to go.

Bumbo manages to hone his tongue sufficiently to give an edge to his voice.

By Christ, it's a braver thing to say we're *not* going to go, because we can't find it in our *consciences* to go, than it is to bleed off, saying, there's nothing *I* can do about it, Jack. It's *you* who pull the trigger. It's *you* who get the bullets. It's *you* who *are* England, who *want* to go there. Don't you see, *you are* England. Each one of you *is* England. And, as for being yellow, wouldn't you all go to *Hungary* tomorrow, if *They* sent you? Why don't you go *there*? All this democracy idea they're fighting for, it comes from us. We've fought for it. We may fight again for it. But we're not fighting *against* it, for any bleeding piddle of salt water, or any bleeding British Government that goes off its bloody rocker.

Sgt. Peters says,

Sir, why don't we let somebody else do it? Why does it have to be us?

Bumbo says,

There's only us. It's got to be us. Not just me. It's got to be *us*.

Sgt. Issy says,

I'm with you, sir. When you say the word.

They all nod, and look down into their beer. Bumbo can hardly believe. So he questions again,

All of you?

They all nod again, and drink in embarrassment.

Bumbo says,

Let's have another drink. Drink to it. Drink, so we won't forget it.

All right, sir, they say. They drink. They are silent. In the coach on the way back, no one talks.

15

MASQUE AS A HARLEQUIN

Bumbo reached Wellington Barracks at nine, to find a telephone message from Susie waiting for him in his pigeon-hole, asking him to meet her at a party at Jock's that night. Bumbo swore. He should go to bed early, because of the Regimental Lieutenant-Colonel's Inspection in the morning. But Susie wasn't for waiting. He would just show his face, take her home, have a quick snog, and get back by twelve.

Bumbo went up to his room to change. He took off his check suit, had a bath, washed his hair, and put on a pair of jeans and a scarlet shirt. On top of these, he put another shirt, a stiff collar, a regulation tie, a regulation dark suit, a rolled umbrella, and a regulation bowler-hat, after smearing, on his fluffy hair, some regulation Honey-and-Flowers. He came downstairs, and went into the dining-room, to find out what time he had to be on parade in the morning. Outram Utterluck was Picquet Officer. But he was surrounded by a group of Captains and Majors, talking dirt, and circulating the port clock-wise from hand to hand, killing time before bed. Usually only one or two of them dined in, but early bed was the rule before big parades.

. . . so, he said, I've been wearing white pants all my life, but I'm still as brown as a berry.

Not Breeches. In the Second?

Yes. Good old Breeches. Great man. So they had to get him away before she could get to her mother. You know what those old Jerry families are like.

He wasn't the man who . . . hahaha-haha . . . who . . . hahaha. . . .

Yes he was . . . hahahaha. . . .

. . . out on an exercise . . . hahahaha. . . .

. . . wanted to have a quick one. . . .

. . . and of all the places to let himself go on . . . hahahaha. . . .

. . . he had to pick an electric fence . . . hahahaha. . . .

Bit of a shock, eh?

. . . bet it cut him short in mid-stream. . . .

. . . it must be fun for the fruits now. . . .

He's never been the same man since. He has to go off to Sister Agnes everyday, and hang it in crushed ice . . . hahahaha. . . .

. . . hahahahahahahahahaha. . . .

And look who's here. The Chelsea Pensioner.

It's good old Bumbo. How are the fairies, ickyboo?

You didn't half let yourself go in the Temple, did you? They've been on the blower to old Belleyes every minute since you've gone.

You'll be marching in, in the morning.

Seven days, without the option. Free Picquets, as many as you want. Roll up, roll up. . . .

Bumbo ignores them. He walks over to Outram, and says,

Outram, what time are we on parade in the morning?

Outram says,

Company Orders, eight-thirty. You aren't going out fruit-picking, Bumbo, are you?

Bumbo says,

I'll be back by midnight. Any news about Suez?

Outram says,

There's a rumour we're getting Marching Orders any day now. But nobody knows, and they aren't going to cancel this Inspection, even if jolly old Nasser drops an H-bomb on the Houses of P. But, Bumbo, you're not looking too good. Do make it back soon.

Bumbo says,

I'll try. I wouldn't want to keel over to-morrow. Bye.

Outram says,

Bye.

Bumbo goes towards the door. As he goes, he hears the Majors, continuing.

. . . Well, what about the Bag tomorrow, to celebrate?

Let's try the Stork.

Let's try the Bag *and* the Stork.

You've got a stork in your bag . . . hahahahaha. . . .

You mean when my bag's through, it's time for the stork . . . hahahahahaha. . . .

. . . hahahahahahahaha. . . .

It was a new funny. Bumbo reckoned to hear it three times at lunch tomorrow and twice at dinner; and, at least half-a-dozen times the day after at the Villiers-Jones, when the Majors had told the Captains, and the Captains had told the Lieutenants, and the Lieutenants had told the Ensigns, and the Ensigns had told the debs, and the debs had told the other debs, who had told the stockbrokers and the men at Lloyds.

Bumbo let himself out of the side-gate of the Barracks, and walked in front of the Palace up Constitution Hill. He wanted to play the sentry-game, for the pleasure of raising his bowler-hat, without looking backwards, at the psychologically correct moment, on the count-one-two-pause after the second movement of the butt-salute, which the sentries would give him, on recognizing his costume.

As Bumbo lifted his bowler-hat at the first pair of sentries, the back edge caught his hair and disarranged it; and he had to smooth his Honey-and-Flowers down with the other hand, before he could slide the front of the bowler-hat back on to his forehead, tilting the hat down towards his nose. Perfectly, the movement should have only needed the one hand. Most annoying. But the ritual was carried out as per Standing Orders at the next pair of sentries.

The lump of darkness that was hanging on Jock's

front railings turned out to be a couple. They were tight.

The man says,

Christ, it's the bloody guards.

The girl says,

Extraordinary. Quite extraordinary. It's going in, too. Extraordinary queer people Jock knows. He always *said* he knew *everybody*, but I didn't know he got as far as this.

The door was open. Luckily there were no people in the hall; but Bumbo could hear the raucous giggle of the girl behind him, and the la-di-dah special funny for the occasion, I say, old boy, could you lend me a fivah? The couple had followed him in, kept upright only by mutual inclination, and the man's hand on the wall.

Bumbo didn't answer, but he went into the downstairs lavatory on the right, and locked himself in. He stripped down to his shirt and jeans, and even rolled up his shoes in a bundle with his hat, umbrella and clothes; he stuffed the lot into hiding behind the back of the seat. His socks were unfortunately black, but they were a reasonable contrast to his sky-blue legs. He unlocked the door, and went back into the hall. The couple were lying on the bottom stairs.

It's a bloody chameleon.

Phoenix. From the ashes. A Phoenix too frequent.

Salamander. Quick-change artiste. No. It's a spy. A renegade. Traitor. Class-enemy.

The male part of the couple pushed himself to his feet. He was dressed in elegant pastels and suede; he was the sort of man who powders between his legs after a bath.

He says,

I'm going to throw you out, throw you bloody well outside.

Bumbo says,

Don't be a B.F. I'm a friend of Jock's.

The girl says,

There. Quite extraordinary. Quite extraordinary people Jock knows.

The man says,

A friend of Jock's is no friend of mine. That's why you always meet such bloody people at Jock's parties. Simply bloody. Confidentially speaking, of course; because Jock's a very good friend of mine . . . intimate friend. But he's got such bloody friends, so don't go up those stairs, because all his bloody friends are at the top.

The girl says,

Heaven, sweetie, is at the top of those heavenly stairs. Don't you listen to him.

She pulls the pastel-man down onto her lap. As Bumbo steps over them up the stairs, he hears her say,

Darling, what was that you were saying about a simply heavenly job in that busy old biz. of yours, being draped in all that heavenly shantung.

If heaven is black, it was at the top of the stairs. In the one patch of light by the window, Bumbo saw Susie. She was kissing, with her usual energy, a tall, fair man with a crew-cut. She seemed to be perfectly happy. Bumbo went across to her. He tapped her on

the shoulder. She did not notice. He tapped again.
She turned round, saying.

Lay off, for Pete's sake.

Bumbo says,

Hi.

Susie says,

Oh, it's *you*. Meet Joe. He's from Stockholm, and he's a real Swede in need.

The Swede bows slightly, and says,

Yes, I need her.

Bumbo says, shortly,

So do I. For god's sake, honey, let's get the hell out of here.

Susie says,

No. I like it. I want to stay.

Bumbo says,

It's important. I must see you alone for a bit.

Susie flicks her head, and pulls a face. She says,

It's always so important for *you*. Why isn't it always so important for everybody else? Why do you always have to come and spoil parties for me?

Bumbo says,

It really *is* important. You may not be seeing me again.

Susie flicks her head again, and says,

Oh, another bit of dramatics. All right. I'll come for a bit, then.

See you, she says over her shoulder to the Swede, not bothering to look back at him. She comes with Bumbo across the landing. Three doors face them. Bumbo tries the first. It is a bedroom, and occupied.

He tries the second. It is a bathroom, unoccupied. He takes Susie inside, and locks the door.

Susie says,

Do we have to sit in here?

Bumbo sits on the edge of the bath. Susie stands by the basin. Bumbo says,

It's the only place where we can get a bit of peace and quiet. Darling, don't be so cross. It's only for ten minutes.

Susie says,

Oh, all right. What is it? Oh, look, my finger-nail's all peeling, and I only put it on this evening. Damn.

She begins scratching off the nail-varnish with the forefinger of the other hand.

Bumbo says,

They may be sending off our battalion to Suez any moment, and I'm not going to go.

Susie says,

Why? Are you staying behind to keep the girls happy, or something?

Bumbo says,

No. I'm going to refuse to go. Conscientiously object. They'll probably put me in jail.

Susie says,

Off you go again. Can't you be normal for a change? Why do you have to be such a hero? Anyway, it'll all be over by the time you get there.

Bumbo says,

You know me, Susie. You must know me by now. You know I've got to do what I think is right.

Susie says,

O.K. Who are you trying to convince, yourself or me? Do it, if you feel you've got to do it. Don't, if you don't. Oh, blast, *another* nail. I do wish this ruddy varnish would stay on.

She begins to pick at another nail.

Bumbo says,

It's terribly important. I mean, nobody has *ever* refused to obey an order in the Brigade. I'll be court martialled, and everything. You must understand how important it is, darling.

Susie, peeling off pink strips, says,

Of course, I understand, darling. There.

She holds up her hand in front of her, looks at it with satisfaction, turns to the mirror over the basin, and, lifting up her face, swivels it from side to side, so that the light is reflected upon her cheeks from all angles. She pats her fixed curls into position where they are.

Bumbo says,

You're not listening.

Susie says,

Yes, I am, darling.

She comes over to Bumbo, pouts her lips forward, kisses him with a sucking sound, wanders on, hums, and says,

Sweetie, let's go and see a movie tomorrow. There's *The Mudfighters* at the local.

Bumbo says,

All right. Let's go. But I'm trying to tell you something.

Susie says,

I've heard. And I've said what I've got to say. Let's go back to the party.

Bumbo says,

Let's go home to you. I've got to get to bed early tonight.

Susie says,

Oh, not now.

Bumbo says,

Well, come and sit here.

Susie says,

Oh, *not* now, Bumbo.

Bumbo reaches out a hand to grab her, but she slaps it away, saying,

Oh, I'm sorry, but you must have noticed, Bumbo sweet.

Bumbo says, stupidly,

What?

Susie says,

I don't want you *that* way any more. You must have noticed just recently. I just don't seem to want you *that* way any more. I don't know why. I just don't. I think what I *really* need now is an affair with a *married* man.

Bumbo says,

You mean you just don't *need* me any more. In fact, I'm expendable.

Susie says,

No. I still love you, but not *that* way. I don't know why. But you're very lucky, because I love heaps of people *that* way, but only you *your* way. We had a really *deep* relationship, didn't we?

Bumbo says,

Yes. I suppose we did.

Susie says,

I'll *always* remember. *Always*, as long as I live. I'm sure we'll have a second time, but not just now. I'm so *busy*, and life's such *fun*. You're not going to spoil it for me, are you, darling? Because I *do* still love you. Do let's go back to the party now, shall we?

Bumbo says the word of power, the irrevocable word, the unanswerable word.

Why? Why did you stop loving me?

Susie says,

I don't know. I just *did*. It just finished.

Susie puckers her face, troubles her eyes, until a tear hesitates, and nearly falls, in sympathy with her mask.

Bumbo says, bitterly,

Well, we knew it was coming, didn't we? We always said it was. Not that it makes it any better, when it does come. But thank you, anyway. You've been a nice bitch.

Susie says,

What do you mean, nice bitch?

Bumbo says,

You always were a bitch, but a nice bitch, a nice, healthy, animal, non-lady bitch. You ate when you were hungry, you drank when you were thirsty, you slept when you were tired. That's what was so nice about you. You just *did*, and no pretences. And now you're just a poodle-bitch. A clipped, scented, hairless poodle-bitch. A poodle-bitch in a ritzy jacket, on a nice platinum lead. A sterile, barren poodle-bitch in a bath of mascara and Arpège.

Susie says,

Well, who started me off? *You* did.

Bumbo says,

Oh, all right, it doesn't matter. It simply doesn't matter a damn. I go, you go. And who cares? It's done. Finished. Caput. But I love you.

Susie says,

And I love you.

She bends forward, and kisses Bumbo again, quickly, on the mouth. She says,

There. All settled. Let's go back to the party now, shall we?

They go back to the party. Bumbo gets hold of a bottle, and sends Susie off to the Swede. Bumbo can't get Jock alone to talk to. Stow it, says Jock, it's a party, and gives him another bottle. After a time, Susie comes back, and says she's going home. Bumbo tells her to go home with the Swede. He's staying. All right, Susie says, and she goes. Caput. The Barren Fig Tree. For both. The B.F. Tree. B.F.

Four hours later, Bumbo was lying on the floor, mixed up in a mess of people. He was feeling feverish. His side hurt to hell. His head was pillowed on something that was squashy and comfortable, but somebody was sitting on his leg, and somebody else was stroking his hand. It was probably the pastel-man, but he couldn't see. Voices were still sounding excited and sincere above him, and hugely significant.

. . . Lucky Alphonse, he's in the middle again. . . .

I mean, you simply couldn't tell which way it was made, but being Boris, either way would have suited him perfectly well. . . .

The thing about Georges Sand was. . . .

Well, with a name like that, poor dear, *anything* she did would be liable to be misconstrued. . . .

Poor bloody old Lawrence. The same trouble as me. A wreath of mist is the usual thing in the north, to hide where the turtles sing. I'd need a bloody fog. But that hanging committee's a bloody farce. Greco, what did he do but lengthen them all out a bit. Modigliani, the same. And I hit on the bloody marvellous idea of exaggerating the bloody source of all life. You can't miss the point. And what happens? Rejected. I ask you. They don't want art, they want artichokes. . . .

Bumbo felt worse. It was all the same, wherever he bloody went. Always the same dirt. There was no getting away from it. *They* got him. *They* got him, body and soul, in the end.

Someone put the loving-bottle of wine into Bumbo's hand, but he could not face the thought of swallowing any more. He felt round for a spare hand in the murk, and left the bottle inside it. Outside the window, light began to dust the dark-grey of the flannel-suited air.

Jock yawns, and says,

They passed an unquiet night and came the bloody Aurora. For God's sake, let's go and get a drink.

Hey, Bumbo, what about slipping us into Welly B?
What about the night tray?

Welly B? What's Welly B?

Jock says,

Wellington bloody Barracks. Don't you
know Bumbo, our gay guardee . . . so gay, so gay, on
his gay, gay way, where the flying fishes play, and the
dawn comes up outa China like thunder and lightning
. . . come on, Bumbo, let's get at the night tray. You're
our last undiminished alternative.

Bumbo had once taken Jock in through the side-
gate of the Barracks; only the officers had the key.
They had drunk for an hour or two in the early morning from the tray that was left out all night for the late-
comers.

Bumbo says,

I don't think it's really. . . .

Oh, Bumboboy, what's this? Ashamed
of your little pals?

I knew he was a bloody spy. . . .

Bumbo says louder,

It's not that; but you see, I'd get Extra
Duty if I took you all in. . . .

A high falsetto recited,

> God won't ask you if you were clever,
>   I think he'll little care;
> When your toil is done for ever
>   He may question, "Were you square?"

The heap groans with laughter.

Jock says,

O.K., Bumboboy, another time, another

time. We'll off to a little place I wot of, char and wad in the square at five o'clock in the yawning, dawning morn.

The heap disengaged itself: limbs returned to their trunks, fingers to their accustomed sockets, pins-and-needles to their owners. Bumbo found himself stiff and cold. Going downstairs, he remembered his clothes, but damn, the loo was locked. He waited miserably outside, until the door opened and a white-faced oaf staggered out. There was a strong smell everywhere; some kind stranger had found Bumbo's bundle of clothing, and had used his bowler-hat as a chamber-pot. Bumbo emptied it, swearing. He then put on his jacket and shoes, and bundled up the remains inside his trousers. Shrieks of derision met him as he came out. The bundle was snatched from his hands. In the mews outside, the pastel-man used his umbrella as a cricket-bat, while Jock bowled his bowler towards a heavy blonde, who was squatting on the ground, with her breasts supported on her knees, shouting, "Howzat?" By the time they had got tired of the sport, Bumbo's hat was reduced to a circular rim, completely detached from the crushed, furry, black cardboard of the dome. His umbrella-shaft had broken in two. Luckily, the rest of his clothes did not amuse them.

They all walked to the square, and stood around, cold and uncomfortable, in the bitterness of the early morning. A large Bentley stopped at the kerb ten yards away; a tall, white-faced figure, dressed in immaculation and a dark suit, came towards the tea-van. It was Belleyes, the Adjutant.

Jock says,

Lawdie, Bumboboy, they're pulling the chain nice and early these days, flushing them out regular onto the streets with us scum, all bright and early. I thought it was the law of increasing returns for the wealthy classes.

Late to bed and early to rise
Makes a man happy and wealthy and a goddam moron.

The blonde says, ogling,

What a treat to see a real gent at this time of day.

Belleyes said nothing, except to ask for a cup of tea. He drank it a little apart from their group, ignoring them. Bumbo sickly remembered the Lieutenant-Colonel's Inspection. He had to be on parade in three hours. God, what a fool he was.

Once Bumbo caught Belleyes looking at him, and he could see himself, black-shoed, blue-trousered, in scarlet shirt and dark-flannel jacket, piebald, ridiculous, in the square.

16

BLACKOUT

Bumbo managed to sleep for one and a half hours, but his servant had to call him three times, to rouse him from his torpor. His side and his head heaved dully, splashing, regular as a seventh wave, spasms of pain into his jaw muscles. As he sleep-walked to the bathroom, he winced at the morning. And then there was the great difficulty in lowering himself into the water. In the end, he descended gingerly, as if his thighs were needles, rather to be balanced, floating on the surface-tension, than laid to rest on the enamel at the bottom.

Log-heavy, he lay in his bath. Two birds sat on his eyelids, pecking through to the retina; they had built their nest under his skull-bone, of twigs and moss, bearing heavy. The water, too, dragged down his body, instead of buoying up his legs, as usual, on the cushion of its warmth.

Bumbo, lying in his bath, shaved with shut eyes; he rubbed the shaving-soap into his chin, and scraped at the roughness on his jaw with his razor. He pulled against the grain of the stubble, until his following finger found only oily smoothness of skin, the texture of warm dough. But he drove too deep at the angle of his jaw, and the sudden feeling of vacuum below the steel, of smarting freshness, made him open his eyes to examine the black-flecked ridges of soap, caught on the projections of the Gillette. Sure enough, the orange mark between blade and edge told him he had cut himself. He closed his lids again, to ease the intolerable slap of daylight on his eyeballs.

Bumbo, clean-shaven, lay inert for several minutes. He then managed to move one foot far enough to take up the slack of the plug-chain against his big toe, so that, with a sudden jerk, he could dislodge the plug. He was so weak that he had to jerk four times, before the plug gave. He continued to lie, while the bathwater drained away about him, until the cold of the air forced him to drag himself upwards, releasing the last gargle of the waste, dammed behind his buttocks. Luckily, the sticking plaster still adhered to his ribs. He dried slowly, brushed his teeth, washed out his mouth, slopped back to his room (his slippers had no heels), put on his Blues, and went down to breakfast. Belleyes was sitting there, eating a kipper.

Belleyes looks at him reflectively, and says,

You were up early this morning, Bumbo.

Bumbo nods, and says,

Yes. I was up early this morning.

Belleyes says,

I was just off to Covent Garden to see about shipping daffodils there, from my place in the Scillies, in the spring. Presumably you had just got up for your morning exercise after your early night yesterday evening.

Bumbo says,

Presumably, yes.

Belleyes says,

I shall be watching you with great interest on the Inspection. I also believe very much in the dawn air as a tonic for the constitution.

Belleyes gets up, and goes out of the room. Bumbo sits, drinking three cups of coffee, trying to swallow scrambled eggs, failing. As he rises, pushing back his chair with his calves, he falls. But he puts his hand on the table, steadies himself. He blinks at the red fever behind his eyes, shakes his head twice, runs his hand through his hair, then touches his side, bites his lip, imagines himself suffering, goes out of the room, puts on his forage cap, settles the gold rim over his eyes, pulls down his jacket under his belt (as a woman her shirt below her skirt), and walks carefully, step after step, across the parade ground, to Company Orders.

1030 Hrs. Bumbo stands for an hour at the side of his platoon, waiting. The regular lines of gold, white, scarlet and black stretch in their nursery textbook formation, drawn up to the specifications of dead soldiers, who used to think geometrically, in twos, threes, thin red lines and hollow squares. Behind the Barrack railings, a mackintoshed crowd gapes. Bumbo looks at them, wondering who is looking at whom, on which side of the bars is the cage; idly he considers whether the prisoner in the Guardroom only sees the Visiting Officer in a wider cell, or recognizes that both are confined within the same circle of their ribs. He closes his eyes briefly to the thought of Bumbo Dying, as a stone dropped in the water, sinking, watching with eyes that drown and dim the concentric ripples open, breed around him endlessly, as he plumbs the pressured deep, which crushes the rings of his bones into his lungs.

Bumbo's bearskin presses in an iron band on the ridge above his eyebrows. He shakes his head from side to side, so that the wicker-cage of black fur, the seven-pound lump, sways and resettles further back on his head, as he pulls with the front of his chin on the curb-chain. He had put the bearskin on, to find the leather inside broken, so that the whole weight sat in a circle round his head, instead of in even distribution over his scalp. The tourniquet tightens. Like a fist, the bearskin closes its grip.

Leaves blow, scattering over the tarmac in the cold of the wind. It is the time of fallen leaves, and of remembrance for the dead. In the Barracks, the prisoners are detailed to pick up the leaves one at a time by hand. They wait under the trees in the afternoons, catching the leaves as they fall. But the leaves fall faster than the prisoners can catch them.

Bumbo swings the balance of his body forwards, and wriggles his toes in his boots, feeling the sickness come upon him. Caught in the backwater of his skull, his thoughts eddy as the leaves, recoiling from the push of the bearskin outside; Buda and Pest, Suez and Susie, maybe mutiny; why so slow, old man, shambling round on inspection, in stooped scarlet?

The tarmac begins to surge like the sea that rolls

in Bumbo's head; his bearskin slips forward. He tries to relax. He stands at ease. He bends his knees. He bites his lower lip. He puts the point of his sword on the ground, crosses his white gloves over the hilt, and leans on the blade, bending.

But all is roller-coaster, in rocking motion. The Inspecting Officer approaches. Farquhar is shouting. Bumbo strains back to attention, sword parallel to his upper-arm. Farquhar goes round the front platoon with the Colonel, slowly, so slowly, oh so slowly. The sky bubbles. The railings warp as if in a great heat, that makes the faces of the crowd melt into indistinction. The tar below boils. Earth is a fiery sea. Billows burn through Bumbo, up waves, surge steam in his skull. But officers never faint. Officers cannot faint. Bite flame from the bleeding lip. Rock. Rock. Rock. . . .

Sgt. Peters, standing behind Bumbo, saw him fall, straight as a red tree, forward onto the ground. He looked at the figure, lying stretched away from him, and said to his officer,

Mr. Bailey, sir, needs the soles of his boots repaired.

17

CLICHES FOR THE COSY LIFE

They carried Bumbo off parade, and sat him in the Company Office. When he remembered again, he could only feel a great quiet within himself, his mind thoughtless and chill as a bottle of hock. No one mentioned his fainting, and he gave no reason. He did not go to lunch, but sat in his room. And when the Lieutenant-Colonel and his retinue had left at half-past three, he went to the door of the Sergeant's Mess, and stood outside. He asked for Sergeant Peters. The sergeant came out to him, smelling of beer.

Sgt. Peters says,

Good afternoon, sir. How are you feeling now, sir?

Bumbo says,

All right, Sarnt Peters. And you?

Sgt. Peters says,

It's that bleeder Sarnt Issy, sir. You've been done on. He's split on you, sir.

Bumbo says,

What do you mean?

Sgt. Peters says,

Sarnt James and me, sir, were having a quick one before lunch when up comes Sarnt Issy sly as a greaser, and he says to us, That Mister Bailey, he's for the high jump. And we say, Blacking out like that, it can happen to everybody. And he says, I'm not mentioning him lying down this morning. And we say, What are you getting at? And he says, the bastard, Incitement to mutiny. Of course, as a loyal subject of the Queen, says he, I had to report it, though I wouldn't be saying anything *personal* against Mister Bailey. He's a very nice officer, but I know my duty. Duty be damned, says Sarnt James, and lands him one on the lughole. But the R.S.M. stops it, and puts Sarnt James on the report, sir. But you've had it, Mister Bailey. It's that bleeder Issy what did you.

Bumbo nods his head. Sgt. Peters says, halting and slowly,

But speaking for myself, sir, you know you can count on me, sir.

Bumbo says,

Shall I tell the Commanding Officer that none of you listened to me?

Sgt. Peters says,

I'll go round the lads, sir, and see what they say, sir. Honest to God, we're all behind you.

Bumbo says,

I'll play it alone. Good afternoon, Sarnt Peters.

Sgt. Peters says,

Good afternoon, sir.

Bumbo walks back to the Officer's Mess. Outram is waiting for him.

Outram says,

The Commanding Officer wants to see you. Good luck, Bumbo.

Bumbo nods and walks back across the parade ground. His footsteps on the concrete passage sound hollow, as though his body already were only a shell. He can think of nothing. He knocks, goes in, closes the door, salutes, and walks to the desk of the Commanding Officer, who sits staring at him, with Belleyes beside him.

The Commanding Officer says,

Bailey, what's wrong with you?

Bumbo says,

Nothing, sir.

The Commanding Officer says,

You used to be a steady, reliable sort of Ensign. You did a lot of good work when you first came to the Battalion. And now you suddenly go to pieces. It's not good enough. It's simply not good enough. You have committed more crimes in the last three days than all the rest of the officers put together in all their service. It's just not good enough, is it?

Bumbo says,

No, sir.

The Commanding Officer says,

Well, what's the matter then? There must be *something* the matter.

Bumbo says,

Nothing, sir.

The Commanding Officer says,

All right, then. We'll take them in order. First, you get drunk on Thursday night, and start a riot in the Inner Temple, causing two hundred pounds' worth of damage. Which you will pay. Is this how an officer in the Reds should behave? What excuses have you got?

Bumbo says,

None at all, sir.

The Commanding Officer says,

Next, we'll take your exhibition on parade this morning. Officers in the Reds do NOT faint on parade. They NEVER faint on Parade. Why did you?

Bumbo says,

I just did, sir.

The Commanding Officer says,

Captain Bounois says he saw you disreputably turned out at five o'clock this morning, along with a crowd of drunkards. You didn't even bother to take the elementary precaution of going to bed early last night. You got drunk instead, and saw the dawn in. Naturally you fainted. You've let the Battalion down, Bailey. You should feel ashamed of yourself.

Bumbo says,

I do, sir.

The Commanding Officer says,

Why did you do it?

Bumbo says,

No reason, sir. It just happened. I just don't know why I do things. They just happen.

The Commanding Officer says,

Don't be stupid. You're a perfectly responsible young man. You have managed to behave perfectly respectably as an adult until now. There's simply NO reason why you should suddenly abrogate all responsibility for your actions, just because you wish to carry on like a spoilt child. Do you mean to tell me seriously that you don't know WHAT you are doing?

Bumbo says,

No, sir. I do know what I am doing. It's just that it doesn't seem to be me doing it. I can't seem to mind that it's ME doing these things.

The Commanding Officer says,

Don't talk nonsense. It's drink. You've been drunk for the last week. Farquhar tells me you started on Queen's Guard. And now we come to the third and most serious charge. You do realize that you are liable for Court Martial, and possibly for hanging, if the charge is High Treason?

Bumbo says,

Yes, sir.

The Commanding Officer says,

Did you think of this at the time?

Bumbo says,

No, sir.

The Commanding Officer says,

Then why did you incite these men to mutiny?

Bumbo says,

I don't know, sir. I don't know that I did, sir.

The Commanding Officer reads from the piece of paper in front of him.

Evidence of Quartermaster-Sgt. Issy. On the night of the 2nd November, at about 1830 hrs. I was sitting in an inn called "The Dog and Duck" with 2/Lt. Bailey and the Rugby League Team. 2/Lt. Bailey requested me whether I

*wished drink with him, and I did not like to refuse him being
an officer. He made several speeches saying that he would not
go to the Suez Canal if the Battalion was ordered. He
attempted to make the rest of the team state that they would
refuse if they was ordered. And they did. But I said neither
yes or no being mindful of my duty to my Queen and country.*

*Upon return to Wellington Barracks at 2030 hrs. I had
recourse to the Manual of Army Orders. I thereby found that
2/Lt. Bailey's words constituted an incitement to mutiny. I
said nothing until 0900 hrs. the following morning because I
was afraid to compromise 2/Lt. Bailey. But when Major
Jorum, D.S.O. asked me to explain certain deficiencies in the
stores I stated that I had a lot on my mind. Upon being
pressed I further stated the above evidence. I explained the
cause for my delay to Major Jorum, D.S.O., and he com-
plimented me on bringing the above mentioned to the full light
of day.*

The Commanding Officer finishes reading, looks
at Bumbo, and says, quietly,

It's a serious charge, Bumbo. Do you deny
it?

Bumbo says,

No, sir. But it's not true that the men
agreed, sir. They all refused.

The Commanding Officer says,

Most likely. We're busting Sarnt Issy as it
is, for whipping more of the stores. But why did you
do it, Bumbo? You know as well as I do, once you're
in the Army, you obey orders. Without question, you
obey orders.

Bumbo says,

Yes, sir. But I didn't think it was right, sir.

The Commanding Officer says,

Right? Who are *you* to question Her Majesty's Government? What do *you* know of the real situation? Have *you* got all the relevant information? When you're in the Army, you do as you're told. I suppose you were also drunk then.

Bumbo says,

I had been drinking, sir.

The Commanding Officer says,

And you can offer no explanation of any of this?

Bumbo says,

No, sir. Except to say that I'm sorry, sir.

The Commanding Officer says,

Well, Bailey, you've only ten more months to do. And you *are* a National Serviceman. We have various alternatives ahead of us. We *could* put you up before a Court Martial, and have you sentenced, perhaps to death. You realize that?

Bumbo says,

Yes, sir.

The Commanding Officer says,

But the whole matter becomes a question of the honour of the Regiment. And you can consider yourself damned lucky that this *is* the question. It's no thanks to you that you're going to get off so lightly. You cannot, of course, consider yourself as an Ensign in the Reds after this occasion, when you have betrayed in the most shameful fashion all the Regiment stands for. You will consider yourself under arrest from this moment. And, at the first possible opportunity, you will resign your commission to the

Regimental Lieutenant-Colonel, who will accept it immediately. In sheer charity, we will ascribe your abominable behaviour to the influence of alcohol. You will never speak of this to any person. You will be officially discharged as medically unfit for military duties. Should the newspapers get hold of it, we may be forced to put you on trial. Therefore you will communicate nothing to anyone. You understand, Bailey?

Bumbo says,

Yes, sir. And thank you, sir.

The Commanding Officer says,

I only hope you realize the full extent of your crime. You have brought dishonour to the Battalion, to the Regiment, and to the Queen. You have failed abysmally as an officer, as a Redsman, and as a gentleman. Your memory of this will be sufficient punishment. You may go.

Bumbo saluted and left the room. He had not resisted. There was nothing to resist. There were no heroics offered, only platitudes. The mere clichés of honour, duty and obedience, spoken in anger by a fool who believed in them, had made Bumbo silent so that he denied the truth that he felt within him. They were all so bloody REASONABLE. So damn FORGIVING, without knowing the real reason for forgiveness. As though HE, BUMBO, didn't MATTER, when it was only boredom that had kept his mouth shut. But, blast it, he was ashamed. They had conditioned him so successfully that their sanctions did make him whimper. He knew that it was all nonsense; that their authority was a fiction; that, in reality, they could not touch the true Bumbo. But he was ashamed.

For, at the time of decision, he had said nothing. Instead of self-justification, he had said nothing. He had behaved as a Redsman should, accepting full responsibility for all his own and his subordinates' actions. He had sinned against the system; the system had condemned him; he accepted the condemnation as just. Yes, Bumbo had accepted, was accepted, would be received into the numbers of the rulers, as an act of charity and social mercy, after he had humbled himself and confessed his faults. Penance was ordered for the rest of his life, the ordered pursuit of riches according to the conventions.

Of course, Bumbo knew that he could have resisted. But resistance did not seem possible at that particular moment. For the very fact of living was the true cross that killed Bumbo's belief in himself, the knowing that day followed day followed day, hour followed hour, minute followed minute, second followed second, sameness after sameness, expected action after expected action in everlasting repetition, world without ending, amen.

18

TWO DIALOGUES

Sgt. Peters crashed into the Regimental Sergeant-Major's Office, and slammed his boots on the floor. The R.S.M. squinted up at him, twisted the left horn of his moustache, and said, as softly as if he were addressing a division at Pirbright with a gale blowing in his teeth.

Sarnt Peters, I've been hearing horrible things about you. Simply horrible things. You wasn't thinking of disobeying an order, was you now? You wasn't thinking of not going to the Canal, was you? You horrible thing, you.

Sgt. Peters says, honest-sounding,

No, sir. Never, sir.

The R.S.M. says,

I'm glad to hear it, Sarnt Peters. I wouldn't like to think any different of you. But a little bird whispered in my ear as how Mr. Bailey put some highly suggestive notions into your thick skull. To which you wasn't adverse.

Sgt. Peters says,

He did mention one or two things, sir. But he was a bit the worse for the drink, so natural-like we didn't heed him at all, sir.

The R.S.M. says,

You restore my faith in human nature,
Sarnt Peters. I always knew as I could count on you.
But why does Sarnt Issy state in evidence that you
agreed with Mr. Bailey?

Sgt. Peters says,

It's a lie, sir. On my honour, sir, it's a lie.

The R.S.M. says,

That may be as be. I wouldn't like to say.
But let this be a warning to you, Sarnt Peters. You be
careful of the company you keep. There are officers
and officers, and it's not all the officers that I would
call highly desirable. It's the Rugby as does it, Sarnt
Peters. As I said to you, you should be playing *Foot-
ball*. That's the game for you. I'll be watching for you
on the pitch, Wednesday, two sharp. So you be there,
Sarnt Peters. You're a horrible man, and you've done
horrible things. Get out of my sight, before I change
my mind.

Sgt. Peters left quickly. It was all right. That poor
bleeder, Mr. Bailey. He was carrying the whole bleeding bleed himself. But that's what officers were for,
wasn't it? To carry the whole bleeding bleed.

Bumbo had dinner taken up to his room. *They* sat
round the table again, still passing the port clockwise.

. . . He's had a light time of it.

He's just a bloody conchie.

It's the same with all these fairies. They
haven't got any guts in them.

Well, *is* he a fairy?

180

Well, he *says* he is sometimes. And if he isn't, I'll bet he's never had a woman. He's never said so.

That's the trouble obviously. He's never had a woman. . . .

(And the sibilant voice hisses),

. . . Let's make him have a woman. It's time he grew up.

Yes, bloody good idea. It's just a lot of childishness.

Arrested development.

What a bleeding lark!

I bet he really wants it, and is just too scared to ask for it.

Well, you've had too much of it.

Too much is impossible. . . .

On and on, and on, they endlessly repeat themselves; always the same topic. And in the round of their conversation, they knot the noose for Bumbo, to draw him finally into the charmed circle.

19

CLOWN AT THE CROSS

Bumbo sits drinking from the night tray, whisky and soda, whisky and soda, whisky and soda. He sits, staring and vacant, the room empty, a smell of old smoke, rubbed leather, shut windows, drawn curtains. He hears *Their* voices in the passage, breaking silence.

... Yes, he's here.

Waiting for us.

Lamb for the slaughter.

Come on, girlie. We're going to take you out, and make a man of you.

Just come along quiet, and we'll save you from yourself.

All the trollops are waiting, just for you, Bumboboy. ...

Bumbo strikes out at them, shouting, Leave me alone, for God's sake let me be. *They* grasp him and clutch him, *They* clasp him and crutch him, saying,

... It's for your good, Bumbo.

Take it easy, now. Mind where your feet go.

Blast, hold the vicious bastard.

Careful, boy, or we'll cool you off in the duck-pond.

Bloody good idea. Let's chuck him in the lake. We'll take him through the side-gate.

Ducks are all *he's* fit for.

Just debag him first, and bung him in afterwards. . . .

They lift Bumbo, kicking, on to the table, where he twists on the smooth surface. *They* roll up a newspaper, strike him on the head, cry, THE FAIRY KING. *They* kneel on each side of him, strain back his wrists, knifed on the table-edge, bone bending-backward. He snaps at *Their* knuckles, bites through to the blood, but *They* laugh in *Their* drunkedness, and jerk at his turtle-head, fingers twined in his scalp, until the roots of his hair are thorns in the pain of his crown.

. . . Damn the silly bleeder.

We're only trying to help him.

Cut him down to normal.

How's the mutiny, Bligh boy? Scared to go to Suez?

What price the Canal now?

Break his bloody braces, if you can't undo them. We'll take him down, rolled in the table-cloth.

Not much to show for himself, has he? . . .

They get Bumbo's trousers off, and sit on his ankles, crushing the bone. Bumbo goes limp. *They* wrap the felt tablecloth around him; the bright bulb above him is blotted out; the felt covers him as great darkness.

183

. . . Hey, let's give Bumbo a drink.

What about some bitters?

Give him a mouth-wash.

Pass the bottle over. . . .

The nozzle tastes more bitter than lemons to Bumbo. It tastes more bitter than being as his sort are. He mumbles, but only he and God can hear his mumbling.

Far voices laughing, in the great darkness,

. . . How much for these trousers? Nice Blues trousers.

What do you offer me?

Two and sixpence ha'penny.

Gentleman in the corner, what am I bid?

Five shillings and fourpence.

Is that all, gentlemen? Going, going, going. Going, going, gone.

Let's play strip-poker.

Toss you for the trousers.

Pass the whisky, Pegtop, and deal me five aces.

Come on, let's go, for God's sake, and chuck him in the water. . . .

They carry Bumbo off, wrapped in the tablecloth. As *They* go, *They* meet Laughing Gus and Outram.

. . . More bloody National Servicemen. They can go in too.

Come on, off to the Park, boys. . . .

They go through the side-gate quietly, so that the sentry on the Main Gate does not see them. *They* carry Bumbo across the Park Garden, hustling along the other Ensigns, who only make a show of resistance to the inevitable, for the fun of their persecutors. *They* unwrap Bumbo from the tablecloth, hold him by the arms and legs, swing him three times, and throw him in the lake. The other two victims wisely walk themselves into the shallows, voluntarily. Pegtop throws Bumbo's trousers after him into the water.

Bumbo sits up, and shivers. He looks at the mocking faces of the officers. He feels pain in his side, where the plaster has been wrenched. Laughing Gus and Outram help him to his feet. He walks to the low shore.

   They stop laughing. *They* grow ashamed. *They* say,

  . . . Forget it, Bumbo, we didn't mean it.

    It was just a bit of fun.

    You come along to the Bag with us. And after that, we'll find you a bit of all right.

     Christalmighty, look at Bumbo's trousers, sinking in the middle there. . . .

Bumbo turns to looks at his trousers, heavy-black as the trunk of a tree in the water. A duck quacks. All laugh. Bumbo laughs with them.

  Sure, Bumbo says, I'll come along.

So they all went to the "Bag". And afterwards some of them picked up women. And Bumbo took a taxi. And his woman did her job, in twenty minutes, somewhere beyond Paddington.

PART FOUR

Epilogue

Who knows whether to live is but to die,
and to die to live?

Euripedes

EPILOGUE

Farquhar marched in before the Commanding Officer. He saluted.

The Commanding Officer says,

Well, Farquhar, what can I do for you?

Farquhar says,

It's Bumbo, sir. With all this bloody stupid business, he's had a bit of a breakdown. And he got hurt in the side from that game up North, and didn't say anything about it. I know he's got a lot against him, but I do think he should get away from here. Just for a few days.

The Commanding Officer says,

A breakdown? Are you sure? It's not just drink, is it?

Belleyes, the Adjutant, from his desk beside the Commanding Officer's, says,

No, sir. Bumbo's not himself at all. I went in to see him this morning, and he was just lying, on top of his bed, with all his clothes on. He wouldn't answer me. I shook him, and he wouldn't move. He doesn't seem quite right to me, sir.

Farquhar says,

If you'd let me, I thought I might send him down to Duncraigie. I would, of course, be wholly responsible for him, sir. I know he should, technically, wait here under arrest till his resignation's through. But, honestly, he's in a bloody mess. What he needs is a complete rest. I'll have him waited on hand and foot, so he needn't do anything for himself. And I'll see that he comes back up here to see the Regimental Lieutenant-Colonel, when he's himself again. I tell you, sir, give him a few days at Duncraigie, and you won't know the difference.

The Commanding Officer says,

All right, Farquhar. It's very good of you to bother.

Farquhar says,

Thank you, sir. But it's quite all right. He didn't do at all badly in the Company, although he's such a bloody fool.

Farquhar stepped backwards to the door, saluted, and went. He sent Bumbo down to Duncraigie in a sleeper that afternoon, and telephoned his aunt, his ghillie and his old Nannie, with strict instructions that everything possible was to be done for Bumbo.

Sheila telephoned the Mess on Wednesday morning, not having heard from Bumbo. The usual voice of the barman answered, Officers' Mess, Wellington Barracks, Sir.

Sheila says,

Could I speak to Mr. *Bailey*, please?

The voice in the telephone receiver answers,

Mr. Bailey's away, ma'am. He's not at all well. He went away yesterday, ma'am. I've got special instructions not to give his address. But Major Farquhar said to me, ma'am, that Mr. Bailey would be coming back in a bit.

Sheila puts her hand to her stomach. She is afraid. She says,

Look. It *is* rather *urgent*. Could you tell Mr. Bailey to *telephone* me, Miss *Smith-Percy*, as *soon* as he gets *back*. The *moment* he gets back. He *knows* the number.

The voice answers,

Miss Smith-Percy, ma'am. I'll see he gets the message.

Sheila says,

Don't forget. It *really* is *very* urgent.

She puts down the telephone, and begins to cry.

Bumbo telephoned through to Sheila from Scotland, and asked her to marry him. Yes, he said, he had really loved her for a long time. No, it wasn't just that he was sorry for her, and wanted to save her name. He promised that he would care for the baby as if it were his own. For he truly loved her. He had only kept away from her after their first meeting, because he had felt a little ashamed and had feared that she did not love him.

Sheila wanted to believe him, so she said, thankfully, that she would love to marry Bumbo. But it would have to be soon. She was sure that she would fall in love with Bumbo after marriage.

After a week in Scotland, Bumbo went to London to hand in his resignation at a last terrible interview with the Regimental Lieutenant-Colonel. He then arranged for the marriage to take place in twenty-five days' time at St. Sebastians', Charlton Place; Sheila's parents had their London house in the parish; Bumbo told the vicar that his parents were dead, and that he was over twenty-one. For both he and Sheila were under the age of consent, and Bumbo feared that his father might refuse to allow the marriage.

After that, Bumbo went home to Penge for the week-end to make his peace with his family. He had meant to tell his father of his dismissal from the Army, and, perhaps, his mother alone of his marriage; for, as he looked round the security of their small existence, he began to sympathize with their prejudices. But his father was so proud of his Brigade son that Bumbo had not the heart to take away that little glory. And, as for his talkative mother, he knew that she could never keep to herself the news that her boy was marrying the daughter of titled parents. So Bumbo said nothing. He tried for the first time in years to show some love for them; he listened to his father's war anecdotes, praised his mother's cornbeef stew, and even drank a third glass of South African sherry. He decided to write to them from his honeymoon hotel on the Riviera; this was the easy way out, the way of no drama, Bumbo's way, the way of the world.

Sheila bluntly told her parents that she was going to have a baby, that Bumbo was the father, and that she loved him; she also added, for good measure, that he was penniless, but of good family and in the Brigade. Bumbo was immediately invited down to Copperfields, the Smith-Percy family seat, for the following week-end; he was duly discreet, vague and charming; in the

192

end, he was reluctantly passed as a possible husband for the only child of wealthy parents. Sheila's mother took a liking to him, and was careful never to leave him alone with her husband, Sir John, who began by muttering darkly of horsewhips and his daughter's honour, but ended by looking around for a sinecure in the City for Bumbo.

The sudden engagement and more sudden wedding-plans caused a great deal of comment in London Society. The Smith-Percies insisted that the arrangements were only hurried because of the overwhelming love of the passionate young pair; but, wherever Bumbo went, knowledgeable young men would come up and say, Jumped the gun, eh, and dig him in the ribs. Bumbo thought cynically of Burning Bushes and Stag's Heads, of wearing horns before he was even married; but he consoled himself with the thought that his life would always be comfortable with Sheila's connections and money. And, in the shopping-afternoons and restaurant-evenings when they were together, Bumbo discovered Sheila's delicacies, foibles, inconsistencies and quick smile. And, from time to time, in his affection for her, he thought that the marriage might work out.

The wedding was the occasion for much ballyhoo. For Sheila was the first of that year's débutantes to get married. Some five hundred pairs of morning trousers, with coats to suit, were necessary for the ceremonies; perhaps a quarter of these clothes belonged to their wearers; the rest were hired. The church was full half-an-hour before the starting-bell; the gossip from the pews drowned the hushed playing of the organ; sixteen bridesmaids, ranging in ages from eighteen to three, and all wearing identical orange-taffeta dresses, each tried to convince the others that orange looked hellish on the remaining fifteen, and divine on themselves; only the bride and the vicar stood aloof, as though they had no part in the proceedings; while Bumbo, unable to cram a tie into his stiff-collar, was almost late for his own marriage.

The ritual began. Sheila, dressed in virgin-white, was making the most of her big moment; Bumbo suspected that her chief joy was competitive; she had got a man, her man, before her contemporaries. But she was also head-high with the pride of the occasion. Bumbo, too, felt that same thrill and sentiment which he had felt on performing each and every Public Duty, publicly and properly; the correct uniform, the right regard for posture and photographers, perfection in positioning, and meticulous modulation of the speaking-voice, with a low I WILL now substitute for a high-pitched GUAAAARD, SHUN. Even the curious bystanders outside stood in two lines up the steps of the church, something in the manner of a Guard of Honour.

At the Reception, Bumbo stood at Sheila's side, while the horde of her friends and the trickle of his passed by to greet them. Sheila's smile permanently advertised her good will and her good teeth; she even managed to talk and smile at the same time, saying,

Yes, I'm *so* happy. . . .

Thank you *so* very, very much. . . .

Very sudden, but I *know* it's what I want. . . .

I *do* hope *your* turn will come soon. . . .

Bumbo, except for an occasional grin at his special friends, remained grave and responsible-looking; he confined his words to a sincere Thank you, varied with an occasional How very *good* of you.

Billy appeared in the line, and stood awkwardly in front of Bumbo. He said, Well, it *has* been a long time, and I wouldn't have thought to see you here, but I'm happy for you all the same. He was trying to sound as pleased as an old friend should, but his words stumbled in his mouth, stiff with his usual dislike of social occasions. Bumbo desperately wanted to tell him why he was marrying Sheila; he wanted to apologize for being beaten, for his weariness, for his loss of pride; he wanted to plead his need for security, affection and a cosy life with a cosy purpose laid down by cosy people; he wanted to joke that a marriage was easier to fix than an abortion; he wanted to justify himself with the plea of deliberate self-sacrifice and humility, if not genuine religion; but all he said was, You must come round and see us as soon as we get back from the honeymoon.

And Billy said, Yes, of course; and he went away.

Marianne and her husband came to shake Bumbo's hand. I hope you will be very happy, she said. As happy as you are, Bumbo said. But she *was* happy, and he did not know.

Jock did not come; and Bumbo had not asked Susie.

Eventually, after an hour and close on a thousand handshakes, his cheek smeared with fond lipstick, Bumbo was free to push his way through the mob. He had refused to make any kind of speech after the cutting of the cake; he pleaded embarrassment, although, had he spoken what he thought of the proceedings, he feared that he might be the only unembarrassed person in the room. His wife kissed his ear, and went off to change into her going-away dress. He threw himself into the mass on a search for Billy, squeezing between jam-packed backs and protruding bosoms, which were straining to free themselves from their prisons of boned-silk. But Bumbo seemed to be less popular on his travels than the champagne-waiters, who never progressed more than a couple of paces before they were forced to return with cleared trays. In the end, Bumbo, completely ignored, became stuck between a table, the wall, and the fat back of one of Sheila's old family retainers; yet, from the distance of ten yards, in snatches, despite all competition, Bumbo could hear the penetrating whisper of his mother-in-law, confiding to one of her friends.

   . . . *Such* a sweet couple, aren't they. . . . Of course, you *might* say they are rather *young*, but *love* you know, you just can't stand in its way. . . . She was *quite*, *quite* determined, there was simply nothing her father and I could do about it, I mean we are simply our children's *slaves* these days. . . . Yes, Bailey *is* a common name, but *Old Norman* you know, despite appearances to the contrary. . . . Yes, he's of *very* good stock, though a trifle obscure. . . . And I'm afraid to say quite, quite *penniless*, though my husband has found some prospects for him, and they say he's quite *clever*. . . . Still, as I say to my husband when he says he's going to horsewhip Bumbo (our little name for him, *quaint* don't you think), *these* days it's not *every* girl who gets both Eton *and* the Brigade. . . . My dear, I *do* assure you, there's simply *no* question about the two young things *having* to get married, though Sheila's family on her *father's* side often tend to have their little ones *rather* prematurely. . . .

At this point, the old family retainer displaced his buttocks from the table, after Bumbo had clipped him smartly on the neck, and had shouted several times, I'm the bridegroom, actually.

The retainer turned round, his hand cupped over his ear, to say, What, what? Speak up, I'm a bit hard of hearing.

Bumbo shouted, I'M THE GROOM.

The retainer wrung his hand delightedly and slapped his back and said, Well, what do you know, I used to be the stablelad.

Billy must have left immediately, for he could not be found. In the end, Bumbo took refuge by the pillars which flanked the large entrance to the room. He breathed, undisturbed. Behind him, the hum fizzled and bubbled, as acquaintances jabbered to acquaintances, and friends could not discuss anything that mattered with friends. By now, all the guests were completely oblivious to the reason for their summonsing. They had been seen at the Reception; they had seen who was at the Reception; now they were grilling each other, trying to discover where they would see and be seen on future occasions.

Solitary, Bumbo lingered by the pillars for a little time; then he walked away to change.

One month later, Susie sat under the hair-drier, turning idly through the pages of the glossies. She came to the Marriage Announcements, and there she saw a photograph of Bumbo, morning-coated, carnation in his button-hole, looking sadly in front of himself, while a girl, in white wedding-gown and veil, hung on his arm, and smiled up at him. Susie read,

The marriage took place on Friday, December 2nd, at St. Sebastian's Church, Charlton Place, of Mr. Benjamin Jonathan Bailey, late the Redston Guards, son of Mr. and Mrs. V. H. Bailey (deceased), and Miss Sheila Anne Gorebroughton Smith-Percy, only daughter of Sir John and Lady Smith-Percy, of Copperfields, Stroud, Gloucester.

Bumbo married? Well, he always was really one of Them, however much he pretended, even with all those lovely letters, and everything. Too serious, really. Gosh, even looking so solemn on his wedding. But he was nice, though he was a bit cracked. No girl could tell what was going on half the time. And that silly row over nothing. And now him married just like that, without a word. Still, there were all the others. Ooh, and sexy old William tonight, calling round in the Lancia. And her dress still at the cleaners. Of course, she *could* wear the black, but it was so dull. Perhaps just the felt skirt, and a blue top, and a cummerbund. And then she could wear those lovely Italian high heels. William was so nice and tall, he wouldn't mind.

Susie turned over the page, and looked at a bra advertisement. She blinked. An eyelash, covered with mascara, pricked her eye. She cried. Black tears ran down her cheek. Blast, she said.

The Rugby team had stopped having a kick-about in the Park. They gathered in a group round Sgt. Peters. Guardsmen Matt, Bart, Andrewes and Thad the Lad, knowing their station, stood a little way apart, throwing the ball from one to another.

L/Sgt. James, P. says,

Me and Bert here saw Bummers the other day. You know, Mr. Bailey. Met him walking along the Mall. You'd hardly know him now. Much fatter, he is. All rich-looking, and dressed up in a black overcoat, and all. He says hello all right, and how are we. And we say O.K. And he says he hopes the team's all right. And we say it hasn't been the same since he's gone.

Sgt. Peters says,

It bleeding hasn't. No one don't give a bleed about it any more.

L/Sgt. James, P. says,

And he says, don't be a mutt. It doesn't make no bleeding difference if he's there or not. We've just got to go on.

L/Sgt. Johnson says,

But he's all distant, like. You can't talk to him any more like you used to.

L/Cpl. Phillips says,

It was a bleeding shame, busting Bummers like that. He was all right. He didn't treat you like a bit of shit, like the rest of them do.

Cpl. James, A. says,

Oh, they're all right. They've got to do their bleeding jobs like we have to. But Bummers, he was a queer one. All that lark for nothing. What do you think, Sarnt Peters?

And Sgt. Peters says,

Bummers was all right. We'd have a better bleeding time if there were more Bummers around. Andrewes, you chuck that bleeding ball over here, or I'll do you, so help me God.